ANGEL CRAFT AND HEALING

Dedication

For my dad, Stanley Bruce, and my grandad, James Richard Heap, who both rest in the Summerland. May angels wing these words to you on beams of light.

With all my love always, from your Princess, Marie xxx

MARIE BRUCE

ANGEL CRAFT AND HEALING

Tap into this vital source of power and magickal help to enhance your life

quantum

LONDON • NEW YORK • TORONTO • SYDNEY

quantum

An imprint of W. Foulsham & Co. Ltd
The Publishing House, Bennetts Close, Cippenham, Slough,
Berkshire, SL1 5AP, England

Foulsham books can be found in all good bookshops and direct from
www.foulsham.com

ISBN 978-0-572-03317-0

Copyright © 2007 Marie Bruce

Cover artwork by Jurgen Ziewe

Illustrations by Karen Perrins and Hayley Francesconi

A CIP record for this book is available from the British Library

The moral right of the author has been asserted

Printed in Great Britain by Creative Print & Design (Wales), Ebbw Vale

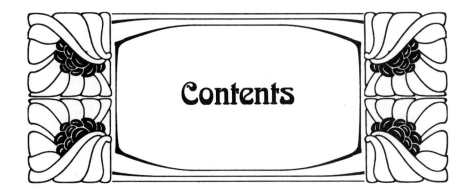

Contents

Angel of the rising star

When you feel your ambitions swell up inside,
On the road to your dreams, I act as your guide.
When you feel that you're lost, yet you want to go far,
Give your trust unto me, I'm your rising star!
When success is elusive and you feel failures blow,
When you're doubting yourself and feeling quite low,
When you feel that your goals are far out of reach,
I am close by your side and some patience I teach.
When the accolades come and you smile at the crowd,
When your name is well known and they chant it out loud,
When your dreams have come true and you shine like a star,
I am right there beside you, to help you go far!

White Feathers Falling

'White feathers falling' means angels are calling. Angels are the best friends you will ever make. They are loving and supportive, loyal and understanding. They don't judge or condemn you for your faults and mistakes, and they never blow you out for the sake of a hot date!

Angels are universal and do not belong to any one specific orthodox religion, although many faiths do carry an inherent belief in angels. Tales of angelic intervention are told in all cultures the world over, and it is widely acknowledged that they serve as a connection between divinity and humankind. Many people believe that they have had some kind of experience of or divine intervention from these powerful beings of light.

Angels are all around us. They are everywhere, and your own personal guardian angel is with you all the time, no matter who you are or what you are doing. You are never alone, and a powerful source of help and comfort is at your side. All you need to do is ask for assistance and guidance, and it shall be given.

Having said that, angels work best with those individuals who are willing to help themselves. This means that those of you who work magick may already have a strong link with your angels, as you spend much of the time in a higher state of consciousness where angels can readily communicate with you.

If you have yet to cast your first spell, it could be that the angels have been active in guiding you to this book of angel magick so that you can begin to work closely with them and heal all aspects of your daily life.

Angel Craft and Healing combines the positive powers of white witchcraft with angelic communication. Here you will learn how to commune with your guardian angel and the archangels. You will be able to explore the differences and similarities between the angels, spirit guides and the presence of loved ones who have passed on. You will learn how to connect with the Gothic angels who can help you through all the darker aspects of life, and you will come to understand the true meaning of what it is to live a healed and balanced life. Whether you are male or female, you are equally able to work with the angels so, if necessary, please substitute 'he' when I have referred to magickal practitioners as 'she'.

Ultimately, *Angel Craft and Healing* will teach you how to bring the light and love of the angelic dimensions into your home, relationships, career and everyday life. Open your heart to the angels and let them teach you how to improve all aspects of your existence. All you need do is turn the page and let the angel craft magick begin.

May you enjoy your uplifting journey to the celestial realms!

Yours in the light,
Morgana

Angels and Witches

ngels are beings of pure love and light. Their light is universal and eternal. It will never go out. Their love is unconditional and transcends all boundaries set out by religious or spiritual belief systems. The angels are available to everyone, all the time, and they are not bound by the limits of time and space as we know them.

The word 'angel' comes from the Greek *angelos* and means messenger. Throughout the world, in all cultures, angels are thought to be the messengers of divinity. Their main role is to function as a bridge of communication between humankind and the divine power. In order for this communication to take place effectively, we need to be open to their presence and their messages. We also need to trust the messages when they do come through and to act upon them rather than ignoring them or dismissing them as the workings of an overactive imagination.

The angels want to work with humankind. They want to help us to overcome problems and challenges and, if we let them, they can teach us how to live in peace – with ourselves and with one another. They want us to enjoy a life in which all our needs are met and in which minor miracles are a daily occurrence – and they are standing at the ready, right now, waiting to help you! As you read the words of this book, your guardian angel is peering over your shoulder, delighted that you are taking steps to begin or improve the psychic link and communication between the two of you. Take a moment right now, close your eyes and see if you can feel the presence of your angels.

Now ask yourself how this book came to be in your possession. Did you feel compelled to look for something about angels? Did a friend or acquaintance lend it to you? Perhaps it came to you almost accidentally, as a gift from a loved one, or maybe it fell off a shelf in a bookshop and, on picking it up and flicking through the pages, you felt drawn to buy it. However it happened, I believe that you were meant to find this book and to learn from it.

I have a theory that everyone who reads any one of my books is absolutely meant to do so. They are destined to become my magickal students and each one has been hand picked by the universe. This is especially the case with *Angel Craft and Healing* as it makes sense that a book about angelic messages would in itself serve as a message to all who are meant to find it. In this sense, the angels have already made themselves known to you. They have tapped gently upon the door of your spiritual self. Whether you choose to answer them or not is up to you, but the fact that you have read this far indicates that at least you have an open mind.

Angelic witchery

Can the magickal energies of angels and witches really work harmoniously together? After all, stereotypes would have us believe that angels are pure goodness, while witches are pure evil. Only the former is true! Angels are indeed everything that is good and loving and pure. As for witches, well, we witches strive to be all that is good and loving and pure too, though this isn't always easy! Fortunately, the angels are on hand to help us out.

The energies of angels and witches can and do work exceedingly well together, largely because both powers work to a code of 'harm none' magickal ethics. As beings of love and light, angels will only ever work for your highest good. This may mean that you get what you need from a spell rather than what you want. But, in general, the results, although surprising, will usually create more harmony, love and joy in your life. Working magick with the angels doesn't bring about negative consequences, so angelic witchery is perfect for neophyte or nervous practitioners who worry that something bad might happen as a result of spellcasting. The angels can guide you through rituals and will always ensure that the magick you make has a positive effect on your life. They will also put a stop to magick that is likely to cause harm in any way, so you really have nothing to lose in working angel magick. Quite the opposite in fact, for you have much to gain.

Over the past few years, magickal practitioners, pagans and witches in particular, have become far more socially acceptable. In the 2001 UK census, 31,000 people stated that paganism was their religion of choice, with 7000 openly declaring themselves as witches and members of the Wiccan community. Even the stereotype of witches is changing as a sexy, young witch-babe comes to the fore, eclipsing the warty, old hag of folkloric tradition!

At the same time, there is a growing awareness of angels, faeries and elemental beings. Angels have been portrayed in hit movies on the big screen, in TV shows, in the work of modern New Age artists, and in the lyrics of popular songs, for example Robbie Williams' classic ballad 'Angels'. It would seem that the angels are calling out to us and slowly, one by one, we are answering their call, using our creative energies to spread the love, light and inspiration that angels can give. To me, it makes perfect sense to combine the gentle, creative powers of witchcraft with the loving force of the angels.

The gift of free will

Another reason why angels and witches work well together is that they are both bound by the laws of free will. This means that every individual must be free to make their own personal life choices. It is for this reason that witches do not put spells on other people in an effort to manipulate them. Instead, we work magick on ourselves, asking that the universal power bring what we need with harm to none.

Of course, free will also means that the angels cannot interfere in your life unless specifically invited to do so. So, if you feel that your life has been a catalogue of chaos and disasters, and you are wondering why your guardian angel has not stepped in to sort it all out for you, then that's the reason. You must exercise your free will and ask the angels for their assistance. You can do this out loud or silently in your head if you prefer. Sometimes a simple 'Please help me!' is enough to kick-start your guardian angel into action.

The only time your guardian angels can act without your request is when you are in actual danger or when your life is at risk. If a situation indicates that you are about to leave the earthly plane well before your time, then your angels are at liberty to step in and give assistance. When people are unable to ask for help themselves, again the angels can act. This is especially the case if loved ones are offering up prayers, spells and incantations on your behalf. But under normal circumstances, if you want the angels to help you out, then you must ask. The more often you ask for angelic assistance, the more smoothly your life will run.

Personal responsibility

The flip side to the free will coin is personal responsibility. Each individual is personally responsible for his or her life choices, mistakes and all. This means that even if your life has every appearance of going down the pan, you shouldn't try to shift the blame on to your parents, spouse, teachers or dysfunctional childhood. As a responsible adult, it is the choices you have made that have brought you to this point in your life. If you don't like the place you are in right now, take full responsibility by accepting that you have made some bad choices in the past, forgive yourself and start to make some positive changes. This book and the angels will help you.

It can be difficult to accept that, for the most part (barring such things as illness, bereavement and so on), your life right now is exactly what you have made it. To a large extent, we create our own problems and failures, and by the same token we can create our own solutions and successes. Accepting total responsibility for yourself and your life is the first stage of making successful magick. And calling on the angels can help you to turn things around for yourself, magickally invoking success, love, joy, health and harmony in your life.

In the presence of angels

So just how do angels communicate with us? How do they make their presence felt within our lives?

Forms of angelic communication are many and varied. Sometimes the angels will send a very subtle sign, while at other times the signs will be screaming at us to take notice. Usually, the angels begin by sending a gentle indication that they are around, followed by more obvious signals if the earlier ones have been missed.

One sign of an angelic presence is the scent of flowers. The elemental devas and faeries also use this sign as a form of communication, as do our loved ones who have passed over. I am sure that some of you will have experienced the scent of a flower or a floral bouquet, which is usually extremely powerful, at a time when there were no flowers nearby. This is the most common sign of an angelic or elemental presence, yet unfortunately it is also the one we most easily dismiss.

When a sudden and unexpected hush descends upon a room full of people, or there is a brief lull in conversation during which no one seems to have anything to say, people often joke that an angel has passed by. Many a true word has been spoken in jest and these silences are indeed a sign that an angel is present. Such silences are not uncomfortable and are usually accompanied by an atmosphere of peace, love and happiness. People may beam smiles at one another and on many occasions the silence is broken by a joke followed by laughter.

The sound of bells ringing is thought to be another form of angelic communication. These could be church bells ringing in the distance, small decorative bells or chimes ringing for no apparent reason, or even the door bell ringing when there is no one at the door! This concept of bells ringing apparently by themselves is perfectly illustrated in the classic James Stewart film *It's A Wonderful Life* in which the ringing of a bell indicates that an angel has earned his wings.

If any or all of these subtle signs are missed or ignored, the angels may then use more obvious signs to denote their presence. Feathers, for example, are sometimes referred to as angel calling cards, as many people report finding them during or shortly after an angel experience.

I remember such an occasion a few years ago. My grandmother had recently passed away and I was opening a package from my publisher that contained an advance copy of my book *Magical Beasts*. I had dedicated the book to my nan and I was wishing that she could see the book and read it, when, on standing up, a small white feather fell off my lap. It hadn't been there before and I took it as a sign that the angels would carry my words to my nan on the astral plane. I kept the feather safe on my altar for a year or so, then I placed it in a healing pouch I had made for my mother when we discovered that she had breast cancer (the spell for this healing pouch can be found in my book *First Steps to Solitary Witchcraft*). She still has the pouch and she has recovered incredibly well from her illness. I am grateful to the angels for watching over her during a difficult time.

Angels can also communicate with us via music, the arts and the media. It may be that each time you turn on the radio, a song about angels is playing. You might be tempted to put this down to coincidence, but if it keeps happening, take note – your angels could be trying to get a message to you. Perhaps you seem to come across angels as you flick through the TV channels, flip the pages of a magazine or stroll around an art gallery. Or it could be that you receive lots of beautiful angel products as gifts. Again, if such things happen to you regularly, take it as a sign that your angels are trying to make contact.

Getting the message across

Sometimes it can take a while to understand the signs that are being sent to us. Even magickal people may need an angelic clout on the head before the penny finally drops! I know I did. I have been working magickally with the angels for many years now, but even so I have been known to miss their attempts to communicate. It took some time before I finally got the message that I was supposed to write this book, for example. The angels were sending me signs quite regularly for about two years, but I was so involved with other writing projects that I just didn't understand what they were trying to tell me.

The first sign came on my birthday when my mother bought me a lovely statue of an angel holding my birthstone. I knew the gift was special and that it belonged on my altar, but I didn't think anything more of it than that. It was simply a very lovely and thoughtful birthday gift from my mum.

A few months later, I was asked to give an interview to a writer from a magazine and it turned out that she was interested in all things angelic. We had a lovely chat but the greater message of the angels passed me by.

One of the great things about being an author is that New Age publishers and record companies often send me their products for free and it was around this time that I began to receive CDs, DVDs and so on, all with an angelic theme. Angels were literally falling through my letterbox in an effort to make me understand. When my birthday came round again and a friend gave me a beautiful crystal angel on a coloured light box, the message finally began to sink in.

In the end I had a dream in which I was told that I would write a book about angels. I have written about angels on and off throughout my career, producing articles, features, poetry and so on, all with an angelic theme. Angels have found their way into my previous books too, simply because I work with them so often. But the dream message was very specific – I was to write a book solely devoted to angels. A few weeks later I signed the publishing contract for *Angel Craft and Healing*.

I mention this experience because it illustrates that we can all be a bit dense sometimes when it comes to receiving and understanding messages from our angels. So don't worry if you don't immediately understand what they are trying to tell you. Just keep an open mind, and eventually all the signs will add up to something that is meaningful to you. Angels are nothing if not persistent.

Psychic communication

Angels are everywhere, all the time. You are never alone, because the angels are with you. But if that's the case, why can't we see them? Why do such powerful beings have to resort to obscure signs and cryptic messages to make themselves known to us?

Well, for one thing, an angel suddenly appearing out of thin air whenever it feels like it is probably not good for your mental health! Not everyone has the psychic capacity to be able to deal with a full-on physical manifestation. You might be fearful of such an encounter, or begin to doubt your own sanity. You might be driving at high speed along the motorway, or using dangerous machinery. In such a situation, an angel manifestation would risk harm to you and to those around you, which would be in complete opposition to everything the angels represent.

So angels make use of other channels of communication instead, ones that fit into our world and are easily incorporated into our daily routines. Unfortunately, such attempts to contact us can easily be ignored or put down to coincidence. Yet, as I have already explained, the angels are persistent in their efforts and never stop trying to get their message across.

In addition to the signs I have already mentioned, angels tend to make full use of our psychic abilities in order to pass their messages on to us. Everyone has some level of psychic ability, and no matter how poor you believe your own psychic skills to be, the chances are that they are much stronger than you think. Your angels can use these skills to communicate with you. Not only that, but they can also help you to improve your psychic powers, thus making communication even easier. The following pages cover some of the ways in which angels utilise human psychic ability in order to contact us.

In your dreams

We spend on average one third of our lives asleep. When we fall asleep, our conscious mind takes a much-needed break and our subconscious mind takes centre stage. This opens up a psychic channel, allowing our angels to communicate with us via our dreams. When angels, spirit guides and deceased loved ones contact us during our sleep, these dreams are called visitation dreams. Many people experience visitation dreams but not everyone recognises them as the vital source of guidance that they are.

Angelic dreams can be prophetic, telling you about something important or useful that will happen in your future. Or it may be that your angels wish to guide you towards a specific course of action, and use your dreams to give you a little nudge. It could even be that they want to warn you about something, and send you a dream that tells you to avoid a particular place, person or situation. Angels may also visit you in dreams in order to prepare you for something that you cannot avoid and to assure you that you have the strength you need to face that particular challenge. We will be looking more closely at working dream magick in Angels of Magick on page 157.

A sense of being guided

Clairsentience is the ability to sense the presence of angels and spirits, and also to sense future events. The angels use this ability to guide us through our daily life. It could be that you find yourself lost in a strange town but you feel drawn to go a certain way. Or maybe you simply feel the presence of angels around you. This sense of being guided through life can be very comforting and inspiring. It can help you to trust your instincts and to go with your gut feeling, particularly if you are convinced that it is your angels who are guiding you.

People with a strong clairsentient ability instantly know when something is not right, or when danger is ahead. They may use expressions such as 'I can feel it in my bones' or 'I just knew something was wrong'. At the same time, those with clairsentience tend to be aware when the angelic forces are letting them know that all is well.

Voices in your head

Clairaudience is the ability to hear the voices of angels, spirit guides and the deceased. These voices may not be physically audible, but can be heard in the mind. Angels use this ability to make themselves heard and to give us the information we most need. It could be that you hear your name whispered softly, or words of comfort such as 'Don't cry' or 'You are not alone'. In moments of danger or distraction, you might hear a voice in your head telling you to stop, slow down, go back or look again. These voices come from the angels and spirit guides, and they will guide you on your path if you trust your power and allow them to speak to you.

People who have strong clairaudient abilities tend to 'hear' the thoughts of their friends and loved ones. They often have a habit of finishing others' sentences, saying the same thing at the same time as someone else and even hearing declarations of love before they have been uttered out loud. Tuning into your internal radio station can give your angelic DJ just the channel he needs to guide you and communicate with you.

Angel eyes

Clairvoyance is the ability to see angels, ghosts, spirits and elementals, and to see glimpses of the past, present and future via premonition or precognitive dreaming.

This is the psychic ability people are most familiar with, yet many people confuse it with clairsentience and clairaudience, believing that they are all the same thing. They are not, but some people do have strong abilities in all three areas.

Angels use the gift of clairvoyance to show us our hidden path. This means that they will often communicate by showing us signs and symbols that we need to interpret and then relate to our own lives. Or they may send us a detailed precognitive dream. Occasionally they may manifest completely so that a clairvoyant person can actually see them in all their angelic glory.

Clairvoyant people can sometimes see strange lights or orbs shining brightly. They may have the ability to see the auras around people, animals and plant life. They are likely to notice meaningful shapes in cloud formations, including perhaps the shape of an angel. They may see a shadowy figure watching over them just before they fall asleep, or first thing on waking.

Those individuals with a strong clairvoyant ability see 'signs' everywhere: in the clouds, in the mist, on billboards and TV and so on. They are likely to use expressions such as 'That's a good/bad sign' or 'I see what you mean'. These people see signs all around them, every day and the angels tend to make the most of this ability by manipulating specific signs to get their messages across.

As you can see from the examples given, you don't need to go into a deep trance to attune with your psychic powers and communicate with angels. Most people have all three abilities within them, although one or possibly two is likely to be stronger. You may be very clairaudient but your clairvoyant skills could do with a little fine-tuning. This is perfectly natural – we can't all excel at everything all the time! And the angels will be drawn to the power that is strongest within you, while you can learn to improve your other psychic powers by becoming more aware of the expressions you use, and the things you instinctively feel, hear and see.

Connecting with angels

Connecting with your angels should be an ongoing process and the bond will strengthen the more effort you put into it. Like any other relationship, the relationship you have with the angels will take time, effort and maintenance. But this should also be an enjoyable learning experience. There are lots of ideas in this book for attuning and making magick with various angels, but for now let us begin by raising your awareness and inviting the angels into your life.

Meditation to raise awareness of the angelic dimensions

Meditation is a wonderful way to raise your awareness and connect with the angels. It is very simple and can be incredibly calming. A silent meditation can be just the path your angel needs to send his message to you.

- ◆ Start by making sure that you won't be disturbed. Turn off your mobile, lock the door and put the answering machine on.
- ◆ Next create a comfortable place to sit. This could be your favourite chair, or a pile of floor cushions.
- ◆ Once you have created your space, put on a CD of beautiful music, preferably on an angelic theme – see the Suggested Listening section at the end of this book (page 201). Alternatively, use classical music, nature sounds or total silence.
- ◆ Now settle down and try to empty your mind of all thoughts. Spend a period of around 20 minutes being very quiet, relaxing and doing nothing but being open to the angels. Listen to the music and let yourself drift on the gentle notes.
- ◆ After about 20 minutes, perform the following spell.

Spell to invite the angels in

Purpose of ritual: To send an invitation to the angels.

Items required: White candle or tea-light with a suitable holder, stick of your favourite incense with holder.

◆ Having carried out the meditation on page 21, you should feel relaxed and calm. Breathe deeply for a few minutes until you are centred.

◆ Now light a white candle or tea-light. Put this in a suitable holder and focus on the flame for a short while.

◆ Next light a stick of your favourite incense and place this in a suitable holder too. Incense has long been used as a way of carrying our wishes and prayers up to divinity and the higher dimensions.

◆ When you feel ready, bring to mind the image of an angel. Try to envision this angel as clearly and in as much detail as possible. Keep this image in your mind's eye for it represents not only your guardian angel, but all the angels in existence.

◆ Now call the angels into your life using the following incantation:

Feathered wings of angel choirs,
I call you here in this hour.
I invite you into my life and pray
That our bond grows stronger day by day.
Angel hosts, now gather round,
May your guidance keep me safe and sound.
Hail and welcome. Blessed be.

◆ Allow the candle and incense to burn down.

Do something quiet and peaceful for the rest of the day. Read books about angels, watch an angelic film, tidy your angel altar, put your collection of angel art cards into an album. Do something that will not upset the calm and balance you feel after the spell.

Now that you have raised your awareness and sent out your invitation, be aware of any small signs that the angels are with you. Over the next few days make a mental note of any fortunate occurrences, strange coincidences, angelic dreams and so on. Keep tuning into your psychic powers and know that the more you are aware of these natural abilities, the stronger they will become. And remember to keep your eyes peeled for white feathers falling!

Red rose knight

Who comes to call when I am low?
Who gladdens my heart when filled with woe?
Who stirs the romance of my mind?
The red rose knight, my spirit guide.

Who is clad in armour black?
Who brings the love I feel I lack?
Who champions me against all foes?
He bears the shield of the red, red rose.

Who kisses me in slumber deep,
As safe my hopes and dreams he keeps?
Who guards my castle in the air?
My red rose knight waits for me there!

Who rides upon a coal-black steed?
Who gives me all the strength I need?
Who brings sweet dreams to my repose?
My spirit-knight of the red, red rose.

Whose fingers gently brush my cheek?
Who lends support when I am weak?
Who gallops with me far away?
My red rose knight, 'til break of day!

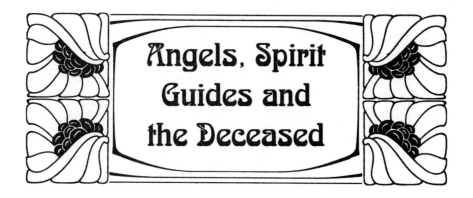

Angels, Spirit Guides and the Deceased

Who are the angels? Are angels and ghosts the same thing? Do we become angels when we die? What about spirit guides, are they angels too or something completely different? These are just some of the questions people ask when they begin to study angels.

Take a walk around any New Age bookshop, browse along the shelves and you will undoubtedly come across dozens of books about angels. On the surface, this is fantastic and it is certainly a positive sign for it demonstrates that the collective state of consciousness is developing and that people are becoming more aware and accepting of the higher dimensions.

Delve a little deeper though and you will soon see that with so much information available, contradiction becomes inevitable. Some authors believe that angels were once human beings, while others state that angels have never lived on earth. Some books will tell you that we could become angels when we die, while others claim that this could never be the case. With such contradiction comes confusion and those new to the study of the angelic dimensions may wonder if they will ever find the truth.

Some authors appear to play it safe and write about other people's experiences of angels. These books are known as testimonials and while they can be a fascinating and uplifting read, they don't usually go into detail about how you can connect with

your guardian angel on a personal level. Other books seem to read more like travelogues with the word 'angel' thrown in every now and then, while still others get so bogged down in the angelic planetary hours and a 'who's who in the nine choirs' that it can sometimes feel as if you are reading a guest list for a celestial party!

You may find yourself asking which authors are right and which books are valid. The truth is that they are all right and they are all valid. The angels communicate with us on a very personal level and our knowledge and experience of angels is always expanding and growing. This means that while one person finds the angels within the structure of an orthodox religion, another may find them in the exotic locations of a sacred holiday resort. While one author spreads the love and light of angels with a collection of testimonials, another may choose to teach the mechanics of angelic attunement and communication. Such diversity is essential because it is the most effective way for the angels to reach as many people as possible.

The personal touch

No two people experience angels in exactly the same way. The angels accept us as individuals. They don't try to group us together or pigeon-hole us in any way. Having said that, there are similarities between one angel encounter and the next.

Most people who have had such an experience claim to have felt an incredible sense of peace and calm, along with feelings of love, protection and safety. Bright lights, orbs, strong fragrances, beautiful music or the sound of angels singing may also be part of an angelic experience. Such are the common denominators.

Yet because we are all unique individuals, the angels will take steps to connect with you on a deeply personal level too. You may smell your favourite flowers all around you; you may hear your childhood nickname or secrets only you know being whispered; you may see a shimmering light that is visible to no one else.

Do try to be aware if such things ever happen to you. Please don't dismiss it as coincidence, for it could be your angels calling out to you. Remember that in making themselves known to you, the angels will always use the personal touch.

Who are the angels?

I have already mentioned some of the contradictions regarding angels. It may be that humankind will never fully understand who or what angels are, or where they come from. I am certainly not going to dictate a specific dogma to you, as I believe that it is up to each individual to make up his or her own mind about angels.

If you believe that your great aunt who passed away before you were born is also your guardian angel, then that's fine. I am not going to argue with you or claim that you are wrong. It may be that the spirit of your aunt is indeed watching over you, and if this is the case then it is certainly guardian angel activity.

Too many books try to pigeon-hole angels – this is not one of them. Who are we to say what an angel is or is not? From my own

experience of writing about angels and faeries over the years, I have learnt that these ethereal beings do not like to be pinned down, and that just when you think they are one thing, they will turn up in a completely different guise and shout 'Surprise!'. What I will do is offer some general opinions as to what the angels are perceived to be magickally, and how they are defined for the purposes of this book. I will also tell you what I personally believe about angels, spirit guides and the deceased.

Elemental angels

An elemental is the life force of a natural energy, and I believe angels to be the highest form of elemental. Angels preside over the heavens and the universe, while the lower elementals, or faeries, preside over the earth and the natural world around us. In some instances, the powers of the angels and faeries work closely together to keep the universe ticking along as it should. Angels and faeries also work well in the magick circle together, with the angelic presence keeping any faerie tricksters firmly in their place! Angels can be invoked within the magick circle or in daily life and they can be petitioned for assistance in any situation. 'Ask and you will receive' is the main message of the angels.

Celestial angels

It is generally thought that angels can be divided into two groups: celestial angels and guardian angels. Celestial angels are slightly more removed from us than guardian angels, though we can still call on their help and work magick with them. Celestial angels tend to be assigned specific roles and preside over such things as love, abundance, wildlife, peace, health, creativity and so on. The archangels that we will be working with over the course of this book are all celestial angels. Celestial angels also act to protect and guide large groups of people working together such as governments, hospital staff, teachers and students, police and armed forces. Their main role is to keep the universe running smoothly, to strengthen those people who are forced to live through chaos due to natural disasters and warfare, and generally to spread the light of the angelic dimensions around our day-to-day world.

Guardian angels

Guardian angels are much closer to us than celestial angels. At the moment of your birth, your guardian angel flew to your side and has been with you ever since. You cannot lose his love. Every person has a guardian angel – even those individuals who do bad things. Guardian angels never leave us, not for a moment; they don't take holidays, sleep on the job or go on strike; they won't fall out with you or leave you for a younger charge, and as betrayal isn't in the angelic vocabulary, they will never let you down.

Guardian angels are privy to the bigger picture of our life path. This means that they have a blueprint or a map of the main events of our lives, the challenges we are due to face and so on. While destiny is ours to determine, I believe that certain points in our life are decided by fate. We are free to make choices along the way, but by the same token, some things are just meant to be. Our guardian angels are privy to this kind of information and their role is to guide us and ensure that we learn all the lessons we need to learn, so fulfilling our ultimate destiny. Your guardian angel can guide you to the correct career path, romantic relationship, choice of home or sacred holiday destination.

Of course, both celestial and guardian angels can and do work together to protect you. The main difference between the two is that celestial angels have other jobs to do, while you are your guardian angel's only job. His sole responsibility is to nurture and protect you all through life and then to help you cross over at the hour of your death.

Spirit guides

Many people believe that they have spirit guides who help them through their daily life. These guides are in addition to their guardian angels. It is generally accepted that angels and spirit guides are different beings, though they do perform very similar roles and, as the name suggests, the purpose of a spirit guide is to guide you on your path through life. Spirit guides and angels work well together and it is perfectly acceptable to call on both beings for their guidance and protection.

I personally believe that spirit guides fall between the angels and faeries on the elemental ladder, being slightly more powerful than the faeries, but not as powerful as the angels. There seem to be groups of spirit guides from particular cultural backgrounds or specific places. Native American Indians, for example, seem to be quite busy as spirit guides. Some people see ancient snake charmers or monks as their spirit guides; highlanders and clansmen also seem quite popular, as do Vikings. Generally speaking, a spirit guide will be connected in some way to your ancestral bloodlines or your cultural roots. It is also possible that your spirit guide may be connected with one of your past lives, and has chosen to guide you through this one.

Some spirit guides are closer to the earth and elemental faeries in nature. In this sense, your spirit guide may appear to you as a dragon, siren, unicorn, winged horse, griffin, sylph or dryad, for example. This is often the case for those who work closely with the land in some way or who have a special connection and affinity with the faerie realms. In some schools of thought, it is believed that elementals work their way up the elemental ladder, becoming spirit guides for a time and eventually being promoted to an angelic status. There is no right or wrong answer. Each individual must make up his or her own mind about such things.

As with angels, spirit guides tend to communicate with us through our dreams, although it is possible that your spirit guide may actually manifest, particularly if you have been working to develop your psychic powers or attending some sort of spiritualist church or mediumship circle. Unlike your guardian angel, however, your spirit guide may not stay with you throughout the whole of your life, visiting instead for a short while to help you through a difficult phase, or to teach you something very specific. Once the job is done, a spirit guide will move on, possibly to be replaced by another guide. Alternatively, you will be left solely in the charge of your guardian angel. Whatever happens, you will never be left without guidance and protection.

Ghosts and the deceased

Some people are drawn to seek out the angels after the death of a loved one, looking for the answers to a myriad of personal questions.

After the loss of a parent or grandparent, young children are sometimes told that their loved one is now an angel, or is living with the angels. This can bring a great deal of comfort and a certain amount of acceptance and understanding to the child. Even as adults, it helps to think that the spirit continues, and that we might still be able to connect with our loved ones in some way.

Personally, I don't believe that angels and deceased loved ones are the same thing at all, though I do think that the spirits of loved ones continue to watch over us and will protect us if they can. In this sense, the deceased certainly act as guardians and so it is understandable that people who feel they have experienced this kind of protection come to regard their grandparents, or whoever, as their angels. Nor do I think that there is anything wrong with holding this point of view, particularly if it offers some form of comfort and reassurance.

For the purposes of this book, though, the term 'angel' will refer to the magickal and celestial beings discussed earlier, rather than to the spirits of loved ones who have crossed over.

Some people believe, and I include myself in this, that on death the spirit crosses over to another realm. From that realm, these spirits can watch over the loved ones they have left behind, perhaps making contact and sending messages to let us know that they are okay and have moved on, but that they are still connected to us in some way. After all, love crosses all boundaries, and it is beyond limitation. In witchcraft, this realm is known as the Summerland.

Visitation dreams are probably the most common way for the deceased to make contact with us. My grandfather died when I was 13 years old and I have experienced many visitation dreams from him. Since that time I have lost my father and my grandmother, and both beloved spirits have visited me in my dreams too. I can occasionally be found sat bolt upright in bed, eyes wide open but not awake, chatting and giggling away with my dead relatives, who invariably perch on the end of my bed just as they did when I was a child. These visitation dreams are not in the least bit frightening and the following day I have full recollection of the visit and the conversation, and I feel filled with a light from within. In my humble opinion, death is not the end.

The angels can help to facilitate such forms of contact and we will be exploring this concept further a little later in the book.

What do angels look like?

I am sure that you are all aware of the stereotypical image of an angel in a long, white gown, with huge, feathered wings, golden curls and a sparkling halo. This image has so captured the imagination of humankind that it will probably never go away completely. Yet a physical sighting of such a being is rare, to say the least, and most people see angels in different ways.

I believe that the angels appear to us as we would expect them to; that they are whatever we perceive them to be. It may be that the stereotypical angel is often popping up in your life in the form of pictures and ornaments, but that any physical manifestation comes to you as a shimmering light, a shape in the clouds or a very helpful, everyday person who simply vanishes after giving assistance.

It is widely accepted that angels are androgynous and can appear to be either male or female. They can appear to be of any colour, race or creed and are likely to take on whatever form connects and resonates most with the individual involved.

The angels are always aware that their vast power and energy might be too much for us, and so they find ways to tone it down and appear to us in less astonishing ways. I have already mentioned bright lights and shimmering orbs, but angels also make full use of nature's resources, and snowflakes and spring blossoms swirling into angelic shapes could also be evidence of an angelic visitation. But it must be stressed that when an actual physical manifestation is needed, your angel will probably look very ordinary indeed and will blend seamlessly into our world and your everyday life.

Of course, in our dreams, visions and meditations, we are allowed to see angels in their most romantic guise – feathered wings and all. But if an ordinary-looking stranger helps you out and then promptly disappears, it could be that you have just encountered your guardian angel on the physical plane.

When people experience an angel encounter there is no doubt in their mind and they are left with an absolute conviction that it was an angel. There may have been no physical evidence at all of such an encounter, merely a feeling or a presence, but when questioned, most people will claim that they 'just knew' it was an angel. I remember such a feeling from my own angelic visitation.

My own angel encounter

Several years ago, circumstances and events beyond my control meant that my life as I had known it up to that point was hanging in tattered shreds. Someone I had loved and trusted completely had let me down very badly. I felt angry, lost and betrayed. I didn't know what to do, where to go or how my future would develop.

At the worst point, I sank down by the side of my bed and sobbed. I felt very alone and was filled with a sense of hopelessness. My safe harbour had been taken from me, I had no money, no real career and no sense of where 'home' was any more. I worked in a job I hated just to make ends meet, and any dreams I had of making something of myself seemed to be just that – dreams.

So I found myself knelt on the floor by my bed, head buried in my arms and I cried and cried, feeling very sorry for myself. I knew that I was alone in the house, but all of a sudden I gasped back my sobs for I instinctively knew that someone or something was in the room with me.

I lifted my head, wiped away my tears and looked around the empty room. Although I couldn't see anything, I knew that someone was standing on the opposite side of the bed, and somehow – don't ask me how – I just knew that this something was an angel. As my sobs subsided and my breathing steadied, I was filled with a sense of immense peace and calm.

I felt the presence of the angel move around the bed until it was behind me, at which point I was engulfed in an overwhelming current of pure love and serenity. In my mind's eye, I could see the angel's wings enfolding me into an angelic hug and at that moment I knew that everything was going to be all right and that it would all turn out for the best. I knew that there was a dark and difficult road ahead of me but I also knew that I had the strength to walk this road

and that I would develop into a stronger, happier and more fulfilled person because of it.

Once the angel had given me this message, along with a sense of guidance, love and protection, I felt his energies retreat. And, of course, my angel was right, and everything did turn out for the best. My life began to move forward quite rapidly after that, enabling me to achieve my goals and become happier than I had ever been before.

During my angel encounter, I didn't hear any bells or choirs of angels singing. I didn't see any shimmering lights or orbs. I just felt an incredibly powerful and reassuring presence. I know it was my angel guiding me on my path and, despite the unpleasant circumstances, it is a moment that I will always remember and for which I am still grateful today.

Your guardian angel

The idea that each and every individual has their own guardian angel might appear to be the stuff that dreams are made of, but so many people from all walks of life claim to have had angel experiences that such an idea should not be discounted.

Many witches and magickal practitioners firmly believe in angels. Maybe this is because we work with various elementals and forms of spirit all the time in our rituals and so perhaps we are more open to the angelic dimensions.

But you don't need to be Wiccan to make contact with your guardian angel and, over the following chapters, we will be exploring various ways to make magick with both guardian and celestial angels.

For the moment, though, I would like you to sit in quiet meditation and try to visualise your own guardian angel. How do you see this being? Does your angel appear to be male or female? Does it have wings? What is it wearing? Is it holding or carrying anything? What colour hair and eyes does it have? Let your mind drift and explore your personal perception of your guardian angel.

It could be that a particular name springs to mind as you focus on your visualisation and you could use this name to connect with your angel. Or your angel may appear to be linked with a particular season or a specific colour.

Once you have visualised your angel in detail, try having a mental conversation with him. When you feel ready to come out of the visualisation, you might like to write down your visions and experiences so that you have a record of them. Then try casting the following spell.

Spell to give you a sign

Purpose of ritual: To ask for a sign from your guardian angel.

Items required: None.

This spell first appeared in my book *Faerie Magick*. It is great for those of you who feel you need proof that you have a guardian angel and that he is listening for your call.

- ◆ Sit quietly for a few moments and breathe deeply until you feel calm and centred.
- ◆ Then close your eyes and say the following incantation out loud:

> *Guardian angel, hear this plea:*
> *Send me a sign that I may see*
> *That I'm not alone; that you're always near*
> *And that my call, you will always hear.*
> *Offer me proof of your shining light*
> *And send me a feather of brilliant white!*
> *So mote it be.*

For the next few days, keep your eyes peeled. Eventually you should come across a white feather and you will know that your guardian angel has heard your plea and is there for you.

Snow angel

Her white-feathered wings gleam northern light,
Her gown is the silver of winter starlight,
Her mantle is moonlight, trimmed with soft cloud,
Her waist-length blonde hair is wild and unbound.
She sings through soft lips, holly-berry red,
Her silver boots sparkle, frost forms where she treads,
And riding her swan-sleigh high in the sky,
She blows snowflake kisses as she passes on by.
She blankets the earth in her magickal down
And the silence of snow enchants every town.
As her white hart prances and his silver bells ring,
We look to the skies and our hearts start to sing!
Some call her the Snow Queen, some see her in dreams
As she sprinkles her blessings and rides the moon beams.
And she holds in her hand a winter-white dove,
Reminding us all that her true gift is love.

Angel Craft

J n this chapter you are going to learn the basic principles of angel craft – that is, working magick with the angels within a witchcraft framework. Some of you reading this book may have come from a magickal or Wiccan background. You may have read some or all of my previous books, or volumes like them by other authors. You may be studying the art of magick within a group or coven, or you may practise informally with friends. Other readers may have no knowledge of magick and witchcraft at all.

Whatever your background or magickal experience may be, the fact is that when we stand before the angels in ritual we are all equal, whether we are hedge witch, third-degree coven priestess or lost soul seeking comfort and guidance. It's all one to the angels, and each path and purpose is equally valid.

What is angel craft?

Angel craft is the art of blending together the principles of witchcraft and the angelic tradition. It is sometimes the very first type of magick that new seekers come across and I believe that this is because the angels are guiding certain individuals towards leading a magickal life. As witches, we try to live our lives in perfect love and perfect trust, so it makes sense that the more witches there are, the more love and trust there will be in the world. Naturally, the angels want to facilitate this and so expand the collective consciousness of humankind.

But why do some people choose to work magickally with angels? And why do witches often call on the powers of their guardian angels when they cast spells, or invoke the archangels when they cast a protective circle? The short answer is because angel magick works well and the presence of angels during any form of positive ritual will give the magick a powerful boost.

I have already mentioned that the angels need to be asked for their assistance before they can intervene in human life. Well, working magick and invoking the angels can often serve as the request for help that the angels are listening out for. In addition, their presence will make absolutely sure that your magick harms none. So that's two basic principles of magick taken care of by the simple act of angelic invocation.

Because witches and magickal practitioners believe in personal responsibility, they are often more able and willing to help themselves than other people are. I am sure you must know people who sit back and wait for life's greatest gifts, all their personal dreams and ambitions and eternal happiness to be handed to them on a plate, without their having to lift a finger or put in the effort. They wait for the lottery of life to hand them the jackpot. Such people tend to complain quite loudly and consistently when life doesn't oblige them.

Magickal practitioners are the complete opposite of this type of person in that they take personal responsibility for their lives, including their goals, ambitions and personal happiness. This means that witches tend to be very driven, determined individuals, who are willing to put huge amounts of effort into achieving their goals and realising their dreams. The angels are drawn to this type of personality as it is always easier and more fun to help those people who go out of their way to help themselves, not to mention being a much more rewarding experience. So the angels are naturally drawn to witches and to those who work positive magick for the greater good of themselves and their loved ones.

The angel healer

People who work regularly with angels in magick and ritual are sometimes called angel healers. There are many angel healers out there in the world, though not all of them would recognise themselves as such. These people are in touch with their own guardian angels and have an acute awareness of the angelic dimensions. They usually have some form of angelic altar set up in their home and they talk to their angels on a daily basis as a matter of course. What marks an angel healer out from her fellow angel enthusiasts, however, is that she spends a great deal of her time spreading the love and light of the angels to others, and she works tirelessly to introduce the higher angelic dimensions to as many people as she can.

An angel healer can do this in a variety of ways. She may read angel oracular cards for her friends and family, and for those in distress or at a crossroads in their lives. She may choose to make her living in a way that involves the angels, say by opening up a shop selling angel products and merchandise, or by giving lectures, talks and workshops with an angel theme. She may write books about angels or represent the angels in a special way, say through her paintings if she is an artist, or through music if she is a musician.

Whatever she does, she will spend large portions of her time introducing the angels to the world. This is the role of the angel healer and if you begin to recognise yourself in the examples given here, then it could be that the angels themselves set you on this path some time ago.

How will angel craft enhance my life?

When you become an angel healer and begin to work angel craft regularly, you will live your life on the cusp, between the worlds. By this I mean that you will have one foot firmly on the earthly plane and the other in the celestial realms. Such regular contact with the angelic beings will undoubtedly have an influence on your everyday

life. You may become more drawn to wearing long, floaty garments, soft fabrics and unrestrictive clothing. Don't be too surprised if you put away your favourite jeans in favour of long gypsy skirts or wide-legged yoga pants! You may also find that you are drawn to wear the colours that are associated with the angelic beings, such as white, ivory, cream, gold, silver, purple, pink and pale blue. Crystals may become an important part of your magick, and you may choose to wear jewellery made from specific crystals and stones. Many angel healers work with crystals quite regularly and may even wear a special crystal pendant around their neck.

In addition to such sartorial changes, when you have worked with angels, you will probably feel much calmer than you did previously. You are less likely to become stressed over small things, and when you do feel ruffled or flustered, you are far more likely to find a positive way of dealing with these natural emotions, for example dancing, running or yoga, rather than destructive habits such as turning to comfort food or alcohol.

Again, this is the influence of your guardian angel guiding you and caring for you. It could even inspire you to take up such positive pastimes on a regular basis, with a yoga class, reiki healing or belly dancing becoming part of your weekly routine. Perhaps you will begin to meditate daily, if you do not do so already. All these things will go a long way to making your life feel more calm and ordered, and will help things to run more smoothly. In addition, you should feel a strong sense of inner calm, and will begin to radiate a glow of peace, joy and happiness out into the world. Such is the positive effect of attuning regularly with the angels.

Ivory tower

You should also expect some changes to occur within your home once you have begun to invite the angels there regularly via your magickal rituals. I have found that working with angels and other elemental beings has inspired me to turn my home into something of an 'ivory tower' where magick and witchcraft can thrive against the perfect backdrop.

It could be that your angels inspire you to do the same or similar. It doesn't matter where you live or how big or small a space you have, any home can become an angelic ivory tower. All you need is a little imagination. Listen to the guidance of your guardian angel.

It could be that you feel drawn to collect angel statues, set up an angel altar or redecorate in pale, angelic colours. You may decide to hang pictures with an angelic theme or to buy a beautiful angel statue for your garden. However it happens and whatever your personal tastes are, the angels will usually find a way to put their own 'ivory tower' stamp on to your home.

As a magickal practitioner, you should treat your home as your temple and, as an angel healer, you should ensure that your temple reflects the angelic dimensions and celestial realms in all their glory.

The power of positive prayer

Do witches pray? Isn't prayer associated with more orthodox religions such as Christianity and Islam? Can prayer play any part in witchcraft and angel craft? To answer these questions we must first asses what a prayer actually is.

The *Compact Oxford English Dictionary* defines the word 'prayer' in the following way:

1. A request for help or expression of thanks addressed to God or another deity.

2. An earnest wish or hope.

Taken in this sense, it would seem that any desire or gratitude expressed to divinity is considered to be a prayer. This effectively means that witches pray whenever they are in their magick circles performing rituals, meditating at their altars or occupied in spell craft. In fact, as most rituals and spells are focused on either giving thanks for what we have or making a request that a specific need be met, it would appear that they are just another form of prayer.

Using such forms of positive prayer in angel craft is the perfect way to go about asking your angels to intervene in your life and help you out. So the more time you spend at your angelic altar and in your circle casting spells, the more likely it is that your prayers will be answered and all your needs be met.

Certain studies have also shown that sick people who are being prayed for by any religious structure tend to recover more quickly and more fully from their illness than those people who do not have the benefit of positive prayer on their side. Once again, this could be because such prayers act as a way of asking the angels for help, enabling these beings of light to intervene.

Lucky number seven

The number seven is considered to be a celestial number and is strongly associated with angels and the heavenly realms. Number seven is ruled by Neptune and is linked with spiritual purpose, higher learning, magick, the hidden mysteries, peace, purity and perfection – all angelic qualities.

This number is deeply ingrained in our everyday lives too. There are seven days in a week, with the seventh day still being considered the most holy. The world is divided by seven seas. The smiling rainbow is made up of seven colours.

Many people consider seven to be their lucky number and perhaps these people are unconsciously tuning into their guardian angel's guidance. If you were born on the seventh day of the seventh month, you will probably have a natural awareness of the angelic dimensions and may find that communing with them comes quite easily to you. And, of course, it is widely known that if you are the seventh child of a seventh child you are particularly blessed.

You can utilise the magickal number seven in angel craft by repeating chants and incantations seven times, or by working spells at seven o'clock in the morning or evening. Sunday, being the seventh day of the week, is also the perfect day to work angel craft rituals and spellcastings. Bear these things in mind when you come to plan and write your own angel rituals.

Tools of angel craft

As with any other magickal path, the tools of angel craft are accessories and are not entirely necessary to casting an effective spell. The real magick lies within you and in your focus and intent. However, tools can certainly help to make you feel more magickal and they can be the visual cue you need to embrace your magickal persona and release your inner angel healer.

Those of you who follow the Wiccan path will be familiar with some of the following tools, though the tools of angel craft are slightly different and it may be that there are one or two items that you don't have at the moment. Collect your tools as and when you can. Ask the angels to guide you to the items that are right for you at a time when you can afford them.

The silver bell

The silver altar bell should have a beautiful high-pitched tone. It is used for ringing in the quarters (see page 61), for cleansing the circle and for invoking and releasing the Queen of Stars and Lord of Light (see pages 63–4). It may take you a while to find an altar bell that you are happy with, for the tone should be a pleasing sound and shouldn't be tinny or grate on your nerves. Imagine what the bells in the celestial realms would sound like and try to find one to match. A good alternative to an altar bell is a musical triangle.

The crystal wand

Unlike the wand of witchcraft, which is generally made of wood and reaches from the inner elbow to the tip of the middle finger, the angel craft wand is made from crystal and is much smaller, usually about the length of your palm from wrist to fingertips. Suitable wands can be made from clear quartz, snowy quartz, rose quartz or amethyst. They may be decorated with silver or left unadorned. The wand is used to direct energy.

The ceremonial sword of power

In angel craft a ceremonial sword is used in place of the Wiccan athame (the ritual dagger used by witches to direct energy), though you would still use your athame to inscribe runes on candles and so on. The main purpose of the sword is to cast the circle and it can also be used in protection magick or when working closely with Archangel Michael. Its blade should always be dull to avoid nasty mishaps! Do shop around for your sword as they can be expensive – keep your eye out for a bargain tucked away in the corner of a New Age shop.

My own sword has a beautiful hilt fashioned to look like the goddess Liberty, and a lovely filigreed steel scabbard to protect it. Your sword can be plain or decorative, it's up to you, but do try to buy one with a scabbard that will protect the blade. Its size should be of a length and weight to suit you – I am petite, so my sword is quite small and light, but if you are tall you could comfortably wield quite a large sword without a problem.

The chalice

The chalice is used for holding the wine used in ritual and to administer potions or libations to divinity. Any stemmed drinking vessel can serve as your chalice, including your Wiccan chalice, if you have one.

The offering plate

The offering plate is used to hold the cakes enjoyed at the end of the ritual, and to place offerings to divinity on the angel altar.

The censer

Incense is a vital part of angel craft as the smoke is said to carry our wishes straight to the angels and divinity. To use incense you will need a censer or some type of incense holder. Censers come with a handle to carry them or are hung on chains. Either kind will do if you are using loose incense and charcoal blocks. If you prefer to use stick or cone incense, then make sure you use an incense holder designed for this purpose as it will catch the hot ash and keep the burning incense safe.

The pentacle

The pentacle is a flat disk with a five-pointed star, or pentagram, engraved upon it. These are easily made at home or widely available in New Age shops and on the internet. If you have a Wiccan pentacle you can use this, though if you choose to create your own, you are then free to decorate it with an angelic theme. Visit a craft shop and use modelling clay that fires in a conventional oven.

These are all the basic tools of angel craft and magick. In addition, you may like to include a set of angel oracular cards, a crystal ball or pendulum, a spirit board and a box of white feathers. Incense, candles, oils and a lighter or matches should also be included in your spellcasting tool chest.

Robes and attire of an angel healer

Many magickal practitioners choose to wear special robes when they are in the ritual circle, finding that this helps when putting on their magickal persona and attuning with their inner magick. Just like the tools listed above, ritual robes are not entirely necessary to work angel magick, but they can help you to set aside your everyday self and become a practitioner of magick and an angel healer.

Having a very special outfit that you wear only for magick can greatly enhance your enjoyment of the ritual. An angel healer should choose robes in one of the angel colours such as white, ivory or cream. Silver is my personal favourite, but you may prefer to wear gold, purple or pale blue. The robe itself can be anything from a long, silk nightdress to an ornate, Camelot-style gown. You can choose to buy something off the rack in a New Age shop, to design and make something yourself if you have the talent, or have something made for you by a specialist company. My own medieval gowns and cloaks were made for me by Dark Angel Designs who specialise in making such garments. A girl I know makes her own gowns by finding patterns on the internet, choosing fabrics and colours that suit her and then setting to work with a sewing machine. She has created some truly magickal garments. So there are many options open to you. Surf the web, browse the shops and see if something inspires you.

If you plan to work magick outdoors in the evening then you will need a cloak to keep out the night-time chill. A black cloak will help you to blend into the darkness and is traditional in witchcraft, but I think a silver cloak is more angelic. A cloak could even be worn indoors as a robe if this is what you prefer to do. Again, it must be stressed that such garments are not necessary to cast an effective spell, but as magick is a sacred practice it makes sense to wear something equally sacred and beautiful, something that you would not ordinarily wear in your everyday life and which you keep solely for your time in circle. Think of it as putting on your magickal Sunday best. I always feel especially magickal when I am dressed in my robes and wearing my moon crown (see below). Such garments can help to put you in the right frame of mind and raise your awareness of the angelic dimensions.

Moon and star crowns

Many witches and magickal practitioners choose to wear a special crown or tiara as part of their magickal dress. A crown is a symbol of power and authority. It also holds a certain enchantment of its very own, bringing to mind images of great kings and queens, and fairy-tale princesses.

In angel magick, a moon crown or star crown is most appropriate and these can be found in Wiccan shops or on the internet. Don't choose a crown that is described as first, second or third degree, as these are for witches who have worked their way up the various stages of a traditional coven, and denote a specific level of magickal knowledge and ability – rather like the stripes earned in the armed forces. Instead, choose a pretty crown with a full moon, crescent moon or plain five-pointed star decoration. Of course, it goes without saying that such crowns should be worn only in ritual, but for those of us with princess issues, magick is a great excuse to indulge in a sparkly tiara!

Angel craft pendant

Most witches wear a pentagram or pentacle necklace. This connects us with our magick on a daily basis and ensures that we never forget who we are and the laws we try to live by. As an angel healer, you may decide to invest in a pendant of an angel or winged sylph design. This will connect you to your angels and will ensure that you are reminded of your powers as an angel craft practitioner. My own angel craft pendant is made of silver and is fashioned to look like a winged maiden taking off into the sky, her head thrown back and hair flying. It is a very graceful ornament and I feel connected to the celestial realms each time I wear it. If the idea of wearing such a pendant appeals to you then ask your guardian angel to guide you to the right piece – then keep your eyes peeled. You may even receive your pendant as a gift. Once you have your special necklace, pass it through the smoke of your favourite incense to bless it, and then wear it every day to connect with your angels.

The Book of Enlightenment

The Book of Enlightenment is your personal diary of angel magick and contains all the spells, rituals, charms, incantations, poems, meditations and so on, that together make up the angel craft of the individual practitioner.

In witchcraft, this tome is known as the Book of Shadows. If you are on the Wiccan path and own such a book, your Book of Enlightenment can form a chapter of this original volume. Or it could be a separate volume altogether – it's up to you. As with any magickal grimoire, it should be handwritten and viewed only by its owner, and it should be lovingly decorated according to its subject matter, in this case angels.

Suitable colours for your Book of Enlightenment are silver, gold, ivory, and metallic shades of purple and blue. Choose a hard-cover notebook, as this will be more durable. Inside, write your magickal or given name and the date you started to keep the book. Underneath this, write 'Book of Enlightenment' and decorate the page as you wish. Write all your favourite spells, rituals, meditations, poems and special dreams you've had in this book. Remember to update it regularly as this is your personal record of your journey with the angels.

The angelic altar

You are now ready to dedicate a space in your home to the angels and the celestial realms by creating your very own angelic altar.

Such an altar will create a focal point for your interactions with the celestial beings and it will also be a daily reminder that you are not alone and that you are being guided on your path. Here you can sit and meditate, write up your Book of Enlightenment and take comfort in the company of the angels. Your altar needn't be a large space, though it should be big enough for you to work your magick comfortably.

Choose a quiet place within your home and pick out a sturdy surface to be your altar. This could be a small coffee table, a wooden storage box, a cabinet or chest of drawers. The important thing is that it is stable so that your candles can burn here safely. Some New Age websites sell custom-made altars complete with built-in candle sconces, scrying mirrors (see page 170), pentacles, offering bowls and so on. While these are beautiful items of furniture, they can be very expensive, and it might be that you could customise an item of your own furniture in a similar way to suit your personal needs. In truth, this is what most magickal practitioners do, making full use of items they already have and creating beautiful and individual altars.

To begin making your angelic altar, lay a cloth of silver, white or gold over the surface. This altar cloth will protect the altar from any hot wax that drips from candles and you can change the cloth each week to keep the altar neat and clean. As this altar will form a link to the celestial beings, you should have some representation of an angel present; you may choose to hang a picture of an angel or a pair of white feather wings on the wall over the altar. Place an angel statue in the middle of the altar and put candles in appropriate holders on either side as your illuminator candles. Add any angel craft tools that you have collected so far and arrange the altar in a way that you find pleasing. Add a lectern to hold open the pages of your spell books when your hands are busy with spell craft.

Do make sure that you find ways to express your personality through your altar. If, for example, you love music, you might choose pictures and statues of angels who are playing musical instruments such as harps, flutes, trumpets and lutes. If you are a bookworm, choose angels who are reading. If you have Celtic blood, use statues of angels with a Celtic cross or knotwork design. Also add one or two items that say something about who you are and are not necessarily anything to do with angels.

My angelic altar, for example, perfectly represents my fascination with and love of winter. I love the dark half of the year with its twinkling frost and ice, and I am always especially excited and pleased when it starts to snow. So my celestial altar is made up of snow angels and ice fairies. In the centre is a large snow angel riding a swan-shaped sleigh through a winter landscape. Her sleigh is pulled by a white stag, and she holds a dove in her hand. After spending time at my altar, I was inspired to write the poem 'Snow angel', and this item is the focal point of the altar. To each side of the sleigh stand pewter elven goblets, one fashioned to look like Arwen and the other Glorfindel from *The Lord of the Rings*. To me, elves will always be associated with winter woodlands and snowscapes. Candles and tea-lights burn in snow angel holders and an ice fairy music box stands in one corner. Two winter fairies ride a snow white unicorn into fairyland and a twinkling crystal glass slipper reminds me that dreams really do come true. Incense burns in a holder with an ice palace design, heart-shaped trinket boxes hold spell papers and wishes, and a silver tiara sparkles and glimmers in the candlelight.

Mine is an elemental and eclectic altar, representing all that I love about the angels, faeries, winter and the world of magick and fairy tales. It serves to connect me with angelic dimensions, gives me a taste of winter in the middle of summer and empowers my magick with a sense of enchantment. Of course, I didn't create this altar overnight and it has taken time to develop the snowy theme.

Most magickal altars have a way of developing almost by themselves, and it may be that your finished altar looks very different from how you first imagined it. But it will always be just right for you and will reflect the inner dreams of your personality if you let it. Just follow your instincts and go with the flow. Once you have created your angelic altar, burn tea-lights and incense here daily and spend time each evening in quiet meditation with your guardian and celestial angels.

Onwards through the celestial stars

So far we have explored the theory of angel craft. By now, you should be feeling more like an angel healer and you should have begun to connect with your guardian angel. It is important that you have some form of altar set up, however simple, as the remainder of the book will build upon what you have learnt so far and you will begin to work magick at your sacred altar of these celestial beings.

In the next chapter you will learn the basic magickal techniques of angel craft and ritual, and you will discover how to introduce yourself to the Queen of Stars, the Lord of Light and the archangels, so read on.

Dancing angels

Sisters of the wing, take flight!
Dancing skyward through the night,
Our stepping stones shall be the stars,
Our resting place the orb of Mars.
And in the bowl of heaven's cup
Starlight gleams – we drink it up!
And bathing in the moonlight blue,
Sweet goddess, love we bring to you.
Then, clasping hands we dance in glee,
Twirling, swirling, flying free,
Descending swiftly to your side,
To be your light, to be your guide.

Across the Bridge of Angels

Y ou are now ready to set forth on your path of angel craft and to take your first steps upon the glimmering bridge of angels. This misty astral bridge is your pathway into the angelic dimensions and celestial realms. You must take with you an open mind, a generous spirit, a loving heart and the voice of truth, for these are the angels' gifts to you and they are the most sacred treasures of angel magick. We will begin your magickal journey across the bridge of angels by introducing you to some spell craft basics and the first stages of any angelic ritual.

Timing

The correct timing of your magick is an intrinsic part of spellcasting, and the following information will help you to make the most of your spells and rituals. Although emergency spells should be cast as and when they are needed, regardless of the day or moon phase, other spells will benefit from being cast at a specific time, as this will help to harness the power of universal energies.

The lunar cycle

The specific movements of the moon are a complicated science, but for the purposes of magick, you need only understand a few basic phases of the moon's cycle.

New moon

This is when the moon first appears as a thin sliver of light in the night sky. All spells for new ventures, new projects and new beginnings should be cast during this phase. The new moon is also good for spells concerning innocence and childhood, and for general cleansings.

Waxing moon

This is the time when the moon grows from new to full. The light gradually increases, appearing to spread from right to left. All spells that work to bring something into your life should be performed during this phase. It is particularly good for spells related to growth and fertility.

Full moon

This phase, when all of the moon is visible, is the most powerful, and all spells can be cast effectively at this time. The night before and the night after the full moon are considered just as potent, giving three whole nights of full-moon power.

Waning moon

This is the time when the moon grows smaller in the sky, appearing to shrink from right to left. Witches use this phase to cast spells that remove unhelpful influences from their lives. These influences may range from poverty and bad habits to bad relationships and negative people. If you want to rid your life of something gently, then work at the time of the waning moon.

Dark moon

The moon is said to be dark when it isn't visible in the sky, usually two or three nights prior to the new moon. This is traditionally a time of rest, and the only magick worked during this phase is banishings (which pull someone or something away from you) and bindings (which freeze someone's or something's influence over you).

Blue moon

A blue moon occurs when there is more than one full moon within a single calendar month. This only happens once every few years, hence the expression 'once in a blue moon'. This is a time for setting long-term goals and for casting spells to manifest your dreams. Blue-moon energy is rare and should never be wasted – you should always work some kind of goal-setting magick on this night.

Magickal colours

Different colours have their own magickal symbolisms and uses in spellcastings.

◆ **Black:** Strong banishings, bindings, limitations, loss, confusion, defining boundaries.
◆ **Blue:** Healing, wisdom, knowledge and dreams.
◆ **Brown:** Neutrality, stability, strength, grace, decision-making, pets, family.
◆ **Gold:** Masculinity, sun power, daylight hours, riches, the god.
◆ **Green:** Finances, security, employment, career, fertility, luck.
◆ **Grey:** Cancellations, anger, greed, envy.

- **Light blue:** Calm, tranquillity, patience, understanding, good health.
- **Orange:** Adaptability, zest for life, energy, imagination.
- **Pink:** Honour, friendship, virtue, morality, success, contentment, self-love, chastity, romance.
- **Purple:** Power, mild banishings, ambition, inner strength, divination.
- **Red:** Love, valour, courage in adversity, allure, passion, sexual energy.
- **Silver:** Femininity, moon power, the night, the goddess.
- **White:** Purity, innocence, cleansings, childhood, truth, protection.
- **Yellow:** Communication, creativity, attraction, examinations, tests.

Remember that these colour correspondences can be related to ribbons, thread, balloons, crayons, paints, candles, glitter and anything else you use in your spellcastings. There are many tools available to include in your magick – just use your imagination.

Angelic ritual bath

Most magickal practitioners and witches tend to cleanse and purify themselves before casting the circle and working magick. Because magick involves communicating with the divine, you should always take steps to be as pure as you can be when in circle. This purification is usually achieved by taking a ritual bath.

Run your bath as normal but do not add any foam, bubbles or bath salts. Instead, add three drops each of vanilla and sandalwood essential oils. Both these oils are associated with the celestial beings and can help to raise your awareness of the angels. Next add about a tablespoon of fine sea salt for cleansing.

For a really magickal bath, float flower heads and petals on the water, light scented candles and play soft angel music. As you bathe, visualise all the stresses and impurities of the day being cleansed from your mind, body and spirit, leaving you uplifted, relaxed and ready to meet the angels and divinity in circle.

After your bath, towel dry and dress in your ritual robes, crown and angel pendant. Having stepped into your angel healer persona, you should feel ready to make magick, so collect all that you need and set up your altar for your chosen spell craft. Finally, light the incense and illuminator candles.

Angelic circle casting

The next stage is to cast your circle, which is a sacred space incorporating your altar and angel craft tools.

◆ Walk deosil (clockwise) in a circle around your chosen space, holding your sword of power out before you. If the space is small, turn in the same direction. If you don't yet have a ritual sword, point with your finger, or use a wand or athame instead.

◆ Visualise a bright white light coming from the point of the sword and creating a sacred circle around you. This light expands to form a bubble that surrounds you.

◆ As you walk around the circle, say:

Celestial angels now flying round,
Each casts a white feather to the ground.
I cast this circle, strong and true,
May angels guide the magick I do.
Outside of time, outside of space,
This circle is sealed with angel grace.
So mote it be.

◆ Your angel circle is now cast and you should cleanse and purify the space by sprinkling a solution of spring water and sea salt around the circle. You may also wish to define your space by scattering white feathers around the perimeter of the circle.

Ringing in the angelic quarters

Next you need to invoke the four archangels at the compass points of your circle. This is known as calling the quarters. In this instance, you are going to ring in the quarters using the altar bell.

◆ Stand in your circle and face north.
◆ Ring the bell three times and say:

> *I call on Uriel, angel of the north,*
> *Angel of magick and dreams, protector of witches.*
> *I call you here to guard and protect this sacred space.*

◆ Now face east, ring the bell three times and say:

> *I call on Raphael, angel of the east,*
> *Light bearer and divine healer.*
> *I call you here to guard and protect this sacred space.*

◆ Now face south, ring the bell three times and say:

> *I call on Michael, angel of the south,*
> *Angel of justice, valour and strength.*
> *I call you here to guard and protect this sacred space.*

◆ Finally face west, ring the bell three times and say:

> *I call on Gabriel, angel of the west,*
> *Protector of women and children, bringing peace to all.*
> *I call you here to guard and protect this sacred space.*

Your circle is now guarded on all sides by the power of the angels.

Ringing in the Bohemian angels

Here is another example of an angelic quarter call, this time inspired by the Bohemian principles of beauty, truth, love and freedom – all angelic qualities. It is performed in exactly the same way as the previous quarter call, using your visualisation skills to imagine these angels as you ring them into your circle.

◆ Stand in your circle facing north. Ring the bell three times and say:

I call on the Angel of Beauty,
Angel of loveliness and grace.
I call you here to guard and protect my sacred space.

◆ Now face east, ring the bell three times and say:

I call on the Angel of Truth,
Angel of honesty, revealer of lies.
I call you here to guard and protect my sacred space.

◆ Next face south, ring the bell three times and say:

I call on the Angel of Love,
Angel of passion and tender feelings.
I call you here to guard and protect my sacred space.

◆ Finally face west, ring the bell three times and say:

I call on the Angel of Freedom,
Angel of independence and liberty.
I call you here to guard and protect my sacred space.

Your circle is now protected by the Bohemian angels.

Once you have performed your chosen quarter call you are ready to invoke divinity into your sacred space.

The Queen of Stars

In my own style of angel craft, I refer to the great goddess as the Queen of Stars. She is the mother of all life, the celestial sovereign lady. Her presence is usually invoked into the magick circle to lend power to your spells and rituals. Her energies are strong yet gentle, so she is in perfect tune with the angelic energies with which you will be working. You can attune with her best by meditating on the night sky, or by working your magickal ritual out of doors in the evening. She is invoked once the circle has been cast and the quarters called. You can use the incantation below, write your own words of invocation or say whatever feels right in the moment.

To invoke the Queen of Stars

◆ Ring your altar bell three times and say:

> *Queen of Stars, angel friend,*
> *I call you here your power to lend.*
> *I invoke you to my circle round,*
> *Where magick is made and spells unbound.*
> *I call you here on beams of light,*
> *Queen of Stars, Queen of Night.*

◆ Stand in silence for a moment and then go on to invoke the Lord of Light.

The Lord of Light

This is another name for the witch's god. He is the seed of all life, the bright sunlight in the sky and the vibrant energy of nature's growth. The presence of the Lord of Light is invoked to lend power to your spells and rituals. His energies are vibrant, fun-loving and protective. You 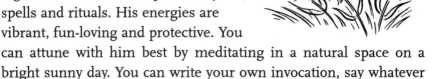 can attune with him best by meditating in a natural space on a bright sunny day. You can write your own invocation, say whatever comes to mind in the moment or use the invocation below.

To invoke the Lord of Light

◆ Ring your altar bell three times and say:

> *Lord of Light, angel friend,*
> *I call you here your powers to lend.*
> *I invoke you here to my circle round,*
> *Where magick is made and spells unbound.*
> *Invoking now your gentle might,*
> *Be welcome here, Lord of Light.*

◆ Stand in silence for a moment and then settle down within your magick circle to begin your spell craft.

You have now crossed the astral bridge of angels and are between the worlds, within your sacred space. This is the time to perform any angel craft spells or rituals from this book, to attune with your guardian angel or to perform angelic divinations or meditations.

Closing the circle

Once all your magickal work is completed, you must release all the powers you have called, take down the circle and tidy your altar in preparation for use next time.

◆ Start by releasing the power of the Lord of Light and the Queen of Stars by saying:

Lord of Light, Queen of Stars, I give thanks for your presence
in this circle. I release you in perfect love and perfect trust.
Blessed be.

◆ Ring the altar bell twice.

◆ You should then release the quarters in reverse order, starting in the west. Go around the circle, saying:

Angel, I release you and give you thanks. Blessed be.

◆ Ring the bell once to close each quarter and then move on to the next.

◆ You should then take down the circle by turning widdershins (anti-clockwise) with your sword, visualising the light being drawn back into the blade and saying:

The circle is open, never broken.
In angel grace, the spell is spoken.

◆ Then clear away so that your altar space is neat and tidy again. This will help to bring your mind back across the bridge of angels and into the everyday world once more.

◆ If you wish to leave offerings of cakes and wine for divinity, now is the time to place them on your altar.

◆ Finally ground your energies by eating and drinking something to re-balance your internal energies. In witchcraft, this is known as the partaking of cakes and ale.

In general, this standard routine should be followed each time you perform a ritual, though different witches and magickal groups will have slight variations in their order of proceedings, some preferring, for instance, to have cakes and ale while still in circle. Find the way that suits you best and go with that.

The archangels

Throughout the course of this book we will be working with six archangels, plus the Gothic angels. You will come to know each one in more detail as you move through the various chapters, but for now here is a brief introduction to each.

- **Archangel Raphael:** Raphael is the healing angel. He is patron of the medical profession and can send healing energies to anything from a broken bone to a broken heart.

- **Gothic angels:** The Gothic angels are drawn to sadness, disease and sorrow because they know that they can help to free us from such things. These angels can help you to deal with death, illness, depression and so on, and they can lead you forward into the light so that you may begin to enjoy life again.

- **Archangel Gabriel:** Gabriel is the angel of love. She is the patron of all women and children, and she wraps them in her gentle protection. She can help to bring love into your life, improve relationships, increase romance and help with all feminine issues.

- **Archangel Michael:** Michael is the great warrior angel, bringing strength and protection to all in need. He is patron of the police and armed forces and he can bring justice to wrongdoers.

- **Archangel Barakiel:** Barakiel is the angel of abundance and success. He is patron of banks and financial services and he also nurtures the abundance of the earth. He can help you with all your financial difficulties and can lead you into a life of plenty.

◆ **Archangel Uriel:** Uriel is the angel of magick and dreams. He is patron of all witches and magickal practitioners who use their powers for positive reasons and the greater good. He can help you to develop your psychic skills and magickal abilities, leading you forward into a life of pure enchantment.

◆ **Archangel Jophiel:** Jophiel is the angel of inspiration. She is patron to all schools of learning and to those who work within the Arts and Performance Arts. She can help you to free your inspiration and creativity and develop your personal talents.

Following the feathers

You are now in a position to follow the feathers of angel craft and move deeper into the celestial realms of magick. Work your way through the chapters, picking and choosing the spells and rituals that resonate with you the most. Feel free to change or adapt these rituals to suit your circumstances, and eventually to write your own angel rituals and poems. In this way, you will create an angel craft tradition that is just right for you and your needs; one that is unique to you and which will help you to grow and develop magickally, spiritually and personally. Remember to record your magickal journey with the angels in your Book of Enlightenment so that you have a personal point of reference.

Angel of comfort

I am the hand you feel on your shoulder
Although you are all alone.
I am the warmth and peace
That surrounds and protects your home.
I am the giggle that bubbles through tears
Even though you are sad and blue.
And in dark of night when you're frozen in fright,
I wrap my wings around you.
I am the hope that lifts your spirit
When everything gets too much.
I am the breeze that caresses your skin
When you long for a comforting touch.
I am the voice that whispers,
Telling you everything will be all right.
I give you the wings to rise above,
I counsel you through your plight.
Mine is the might that strengthens you
And keeps you from falling apart.
I am the love you long for
When loneliness fills your heart.
Mine is the hand you reach out for
When stretching into thin air.
I am the help you cry out for.
Know that I will always be there.

Healing Angels

One of the most powerful magickal acts you will ever perform with the angels is that of healing. The loving energies of the celestial beings will help you to heal all aspects of your life and bring about a state of overall balance. When our lives are out of balance, we tend to suffer for it. We may become ill, stressed, depressed, over or under weight; we may even develop an addiction of some kind. As always, the angels are on hand to help out.

Healing and curing

When people think of healing, they tend to imagine an immediate cure-all. It is true that some things can be healed more quickly than others, but nothing is ever instantaneous – not even magick.

When witches and magickal practitioners talk about healing, they usually mean the restoring of balance and serenity to a particular person or situation. Not all healing is medicinal, and the greater part of a witch's healing work revolves around life issues. The healing of illness is the job of a medical professional; a witch spends much of her time healing poor relationships, stagnant careers and dire personal finances.

Of course, some witches do perform healing rituals when their loved ones are sick, but this should never be confused with a cure. While a healing spell can be performed to offer a sick person love, comfort and strength, this is not the same as curing the illness. And it goes without saying that all healing rituals should be performed in conjunction with conventional medicine, not instead of it.

Say, for example, that a loved one needs to undergo life-saving surgery, chemotherapy or dialysis treatments; in such circumstances, a healing ritual can help the sick person to endure the treatment and give the strength needed to fight the illness. In addition, the knowledge that a little white healing magick is being performed on his or her behalf can help the sick person remain positive without offering false hope. Think back to what was said earlier about spells being a form of prayer, and consider the effect positive prayer can have on the recovery rate of those who are ill. So, although healing magick is not a cure, it can certainly be used to good effect.

No magickal practitioner should ever claim to have the power to cure anything. This book is not about curing – it is about healing. That is, restoring balance to all aspects of life.

Life is in the balance

So, how do you know if your life is out of balance? And what does any sort of unbalance mean for your day-to-day existence?

Nobody's life ever becomes seriously unbalanced over night. It is a gradual process. This can mean, however, that we barely notice the change until something major happens to give us a jolt.

You already know that the angels communicate with you using various signs and cryptic messages. So, there will always have been a few signs to let you know that something needs to change in your life, before the worst happens. One of the main functions of your guardian angel is to warn you when you are about to make a mistake, or even go off the rails completely. The more in tune you are with the celestial realms, the more likely it is that you will hear this warning and take notice.

Have you ever heard someone use the expression 'I could hear the alarm bells ringing in my head'? Maybe you have had cause to

use the expression yourself – I know I have. These m
bells are a sign from your angels that something is n
It could be that you are about to make an avoidable
the wrong person or make a foolish life choice. When you hear
those mental bells ring, go carefully through that aspect of your life.
What are you being warned about? Listen out for the guidance of
your angels. They won't lead you astray.

Other signs that your life is out of balance are addictions, eating
disorders, spiralling debts, depression, anger-management
problems, lifestyle-related illness, a feeling of living in constant
chaos, repetition of a negative cycle of behaviour. The more
unbalanced your life is, the more healing work you need to do with
the angels. And the good news is that the angels love a challenge, so
if your whole life is a bit of a mess, the angels will adore you for it
and will help you to sort it out.

Working healing for others

Sometimes the healing work you want to do is not for yourself but
for a friend, family member or loved one. It may be that all you can
do to help someone is work a little spell, and there is no greater act
of loving witchery than working positive magick for a friend in need.
The angels will certainly be on board to help, providing that you
adhere to a few simple rules.

The main rule when working any sort of magick for someone
else, and healing magick in particular, is that you must get the
subject's permission to work magick for them, before you do the
ritual. This is because working magick without the subject's
knowledge goes against their free will. Your subject must actively
choose to have spells cast for him or her. Once permission is given,
the psychic channels between you and your subject will be more
open, making your job as a witch that much easier. And at the end
of any healing ritual, you must always add the rider:

*I cast this spell with harm to none and in accordance with the
greater good. So mote it be.*

This simply means that the healing ritual will cause no harm to anyone, and that if the subject does not respond to the magick then the outcome, whatever it may be, will be for the greater good of all concerned. Finally, always ask that your own guardian angel connect with the subject's guardian angel as you perform the ritual as this will strengthen the channel between you and your subject.

Archangel Raphael, the healer

Although all angels are associated with healing to some degree, Archangel Raphael is the great healer of the celestial realms. He is associated with the direction of east, the season of spring and the first light of dawn. His most sacred time is that of the spring equinox. Air is his element, so if you were born into the astrological signs of Gemini, Libra or Aquarius you are already protected by Raphael, and he is watching over your path through life. He is usually linked with the colours of spring: pale yellows, gold, and light to emerald greens. Use these colours in any healing spells you work with Raphael and add a touch of light blue too.

Raphael's name means 'shining healer' and he is thought to be the patron of all the medical professions, from care workers to consultants. If you work in the care or medical sector then call on Raphael before each shift to help you deal compassionately with the tasks of the day. He is usually depicted carrying a caduceus, a staff entwined with two serpents, which symbolises the life force of which he is the divine healer and protector. This symbol is still used today within the medical profession.

Raphael is fun-loving, friendly and one of the most accessible of all the archangels. Visualise him swathed in green and golden light, bearing his staff, ready to heal and assist all who ask.

Ritual to create an angelic healing circle

Purpose of ritual: To balance out your life.

Items required: Paper or card, a compass, ruler, pencil, silver or gold pen, coloured pencils, small guardian angel brooch.

Lunar phase: New to waxing moon.

This ritual will help to start the ball rolling in bringing overall balance to your life. Here you are going to make a witch's version of a prayer wheel, one which is dedicated to the angels and which focuses on creating a balanced and successful future for yourself.

◆ Begin by following the magickal routine set out on pages 60–1.

◆ Once all your preparations are made, settle down at your altar and think about which areas of your life are out of balance and which you would like to bring a little angel healing to.

◆ Set your compass at 2 cm/1 in, and draw a circle in the middle of the sheet of paper or card. The circle is a symbol of balance and healing and it is an intrinsic part of magick and ritual.

◆ Now increase the compass setting by 1 cm/0.5 in and, making sure to use the same centre, draw another circle around the outside of the first. Continue in this manner until you have the number of rings you require – that is one outer ring for each area of life you wish to heal. (Don't count the central circle.) Your page should begin to resemble the patterns of a tree trunk, with several rings growing outwards from the original circle.

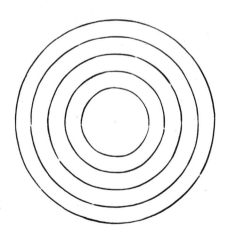

- Using the silver or gold pen, write 'angel healing' around the inside edge of the central circle. Then write one life area in each of the outer rings, for example, health, career, relationships or finances.
- Using the coloured pencils, colour each outer ring in a shade appropriate to its purpose, using the list of magickal colours (see pages 57–8) to help you. Colour the central circle in yellow, pink or blue, or leave it white as these are all angelic colours.
- Now turn the healing circle over and, on the back, write:

  In the name of Archangel Raphael
  And my guardian angel as well,
  Please free me from all trouble and strife
  And heal these aspects of my life.
  So mote it be.

- Say these words out loud seven times. Seven is the magickal number of the angelic realms and so this will help to enhance your ritual.
- Finally, turn the prayer wheel back over and fix the guardian angel brooch to the very centre of the healing circle. Keep this healing circle on your angel altar, or place it somewhere else where you will see it every day.

If you like, you could make several identical healing circles and dot them around your home and workplace. In this way, you will be reminded daily that the angels are on your side and that you are working magickally towards the best life possible for yourself.

Healing chaos

There will be times in your life when nothing seems to go right, when you are faced with one challenge or disappointment after another and your daily existence may seem to be swamped in utter chaos. On the surface, this would appear to be a bad thing, and such times are tough to get through, to say the least. It can also feel as if you have lost control of your life, and you will need to draw on all your integrity and inner strength.

But there is truth in the old saying 'every cloud has a silver lining', and while chaos may have taken over your life, on a deeper level, it is actually doing you a favour. The main purpose of chaos is to strip away all that no longer serves you and to force you to move forwards in your life. Just as a winter gale strips dead bark and branches from trees, so chaos will tear away anything in your life that is not for your highest good.

Many people who have lost their job, experienced the breakdown of a marriage or romantic relationship or been forced to move house, have then gone on to enjoy a happier and more fulfilled life, usually as a direct consequence of the initial loss. This is how the universal law works: it sends chaos to strip away the dead wood of your life, thus making room for a minor miracle to take place. While chaos and change are uncomfortable, in the long term they are usually blessings in disguise, serving to move your life forward and to increase your joy.

No one understands this concept better than the angels. But they also understand that such chaos and change is often unwelcome and that we may need a little help along the way to deal with the new direction our lives have taken. As your guardian angel is privy to your greater life path, he can help to shed light on the reason behind the chaos and to make this healing process easier for you.

White feathers healing ritual

Purpose of ritual: To heal chaos.

Items required: As many fluffy white feathers as you can find or buy in a craft shop – at least seven, box to hold the feathers.

Lunar phase: Full moon.

This ritual will help you to ease your way through a period of chaos and change in your life.

◆ Make all the usual preparations (see pages 60–1) and then settle down in the magick circle at your altar. Spend time here thinking about all that is going on in your life and ask your angels to enlighten you as to the purpose of this challenge.

◆ Meditate on your guardian angel for ten to fifteen minutes. Don't worry if you do not receive immediate clarity – just be aware of any celestial signs you may receive over the next few days.

◆ When you feel ready, scoop up the white feathers and, holding them between your palms, say:

I charge these white feathers with the power to heal the chaos
in my life. I accept the change and will overcome this
challenge, stepping out into a life of love, trust and light.

◆ Leave the feathers in a box on your angel altar and clear away the rest of your things.

◆ Each day following the ritual, take one feather and release it on the wind or in a body of water such as a river. As you do so, say:

White feather, fly away,
Take with you the dark of day.
Heal chaos, restore calm,
Angels bring your healing balm.
The brightest silver lines my cloud,
Let chaos depart and peace be found.
So mote it be.

◆ Repeat this each day until all your feathers are gone, by which time peace and serenity should be making their way back into your life.

Negative cycles of behaviour

One of the reasons for your life being out of balance could be that you keep on making the same mistakes, repeating a negative cycle of behaviour. Perhaps you have a tendency to get involved in impossible or even abusive romantic relationships, or maybe you struggle with time-keeping and honouring your commitments. Perhaps you promise yourself that you will stop binge drinking on Saturday nights – only to wake up on a park bench to the shining light of a policeman's torch.

Whatever your particular vice may be, Raphael can help you to break the cycle and kick the habit, providing that you are totally committed to making this positive change. Remember that magick best helps those who help themselves.

Spell to break a negative loop

Purpose of ritual: To end a negative pattern of behaviour.

Items required: Pentacle, small image of an angel to represent Raphael, inscribing tool, white candle, spool of black cotton, embroidery scissors, candle holder.

Lunar phase: Waning to dark moon.

◆ Prepare for your spell craft in the usual way (see pages 60–1), then settle down at your altar and breathe deeply until you feel centred.

◆ Place your altar pentacle in the middle of the altar with your angel representation on top.

◆ Using the inscribing tool, inscribe your name on to the white candle. Take the black cotton and wrap the thread around the candle until your name is covered. This represents the negative cycle that you are in the middle of.

◆ Hold the candle between your palms and say:

I call Raphael, please circle round
And break the bonds by which I am bound.

◆ Now using the embroidery scissors, cut away the thread from the candle. Once the candle is free of cotton, stand it in a holder, light the wick and say:

This loop is broken, now I am free
To begin again, so mote it be.

◆ Place the candle in front of the angel and pentacle and allow it to burn down.

◆ Once you have finished at your altar, clear away and go about your day.

Some negative cycles are more difficult to break than others, so don't be afraid to repeat this spell if you need to. I would suggest performing it each waning moon for six consecutive months. This will give you the chance to work towards positive change – you won't break an old habit overnight.

Ritual to create an angelic healing pouch

Purpose of ritual: To offer healing love to a sick person.

Items required: Black and pink paper or card, scissors, silver pen, small pouch, white feather, angel charm, pentagram charm, rose quartz crystal, amethyst crystal, lavender oil.

Lunar phase: Waxing to full moon.

Before you begin this spell, remember what you have learnt about working healing magick for others – that it is not a cure and you must get the subject's permission first.

◆ Prepare for ritual in the usual way (see pages 60–1).
◆ Settle down at your altar and cut out two identical love hearts, one each from the black and pink paper or card. Using the silver pen, write the name of the sick person on the pink heart, and the nature of the illness on the black heart.
◆ Put the black heart before you on the altar, hold your hands over it and say:

> *Raphael, take away this pain.*
> *Heal ---- of this bane.*
> *For the free will of all and with harm to none,*
> *In angel love this spell is done.*

◆ Place the black heart to one side.
◆ Now take up the pouch and say:

> *I take this pouch of fabric soft*
> *And offer it up to the angels aloft.*

◆ Hold the pouch up at each of the four quarters of your circle, offering it to north, east, south and west. Return to your altar.
◆ Place the pink heart in the pouch and say:

> *I bless ---- with healing and love.*

◆ Add the white feather and say:

> *A white feather falls from the heavens above.*

◆ Add the angel charm and say:

> *May angels protect and watch over you.*

◆ Add the pentagram charm and say:

> *Wish on this star, your dreams may come true.*

- Add the rose quartz crystal and say:
  > *This crystal rose is a loving charm.*
- Add the amethyst crystal and say:
  > *Amethyst heals and instils calm.*
- Close the pouch, sprinkle it with lavender oil and say:
  > *Lavender's tears will calm all fears,*
  > *Be healed by angels of celestial spheres.*
  > *In perfect love and perfect trust,*
  > *So mote it be.*
- Clear away your things and bury the black heart in a woodland or at a crossroads, away from your home and the home of your subject.
- Give the healing pouch and a copy of the spell words to your loved one – this will explain the magickal significance of each item in the pouch. Write a loving message in a get well card and deliver this and your gifts with a smile. Your healing ritual will then be complete.

Poppy spell for convalescence

Purpose of ritual: To help someone through a period of convalescence.

Items required: Single red poppy, length of red ribbon, small vase, packet of poppy seeds, fruit basket containing pomegranates.

Lunar phase: Full moon.

◆ Prepare for ritual in the usual way (see pages 60–1).

◆ Sit quietly at your altar and contemplate the nature of the convalescence, for example post natal or post operative. If this spell is for someone else, remember to get permission before performing it.

◆ Visualise the convalescing person inside a bubble of pink light and surrounded by healing angels.

◆ Take the poppy and tie the red ribbon in a bow around the stem near to the head of the poppy.

◆ Both the poppy and the pomegranate are associated with Goddess Persephone, so invoke her energies by chanting:

Persephone, Persephone, Underworld Queen,
Come with the angels from the realm of Unseen!

◆ Continue chanting for as long as you comfortably can, all the while visualising a complete and speedy recovery for yourself or your loved one.

◆ Place the poppy in a small vase on your angelic altar.

◆ End the ritual and tidy your altar.

◆ Go to a wild place and scatter the poppy seeds as an offering of thanks to Persephone.

◆ If you are the one in convalescence, eat a pomegranate, the sacred fruit of this goddess, or take a fruit basket containing pomegranates to your loved one. This will connect them to your spell and so aid their recovery.

Spell to bring issues to the surface

Purpose of ritual: To dig deep and find the real problem.

Items required: Small slip of paper, silver pen, statue of an angel (for example one of your altar figures), tea-light in a holder.

Lunar phase: New moon.

Only once issues are brought to the surface and are out in the open can we begin to deal with them and start to heal ourselves.

- On the night of the new moon, prepare for your ritual (see pages 60–1) and settle down at your altar.
- Meditate on your guardian angel until you can sense his presence within your magick circle. Then spend some time thinking about the particular situation that you need to get to the bottom of. If you feel like chatting to your angel either mentally or out loud, then do so, explaining how you feel about the situation and what it is that you need clarifying.
- Write the following words on the spell paper:

    By all the power of new moon light,
    By all the power of angels bright,
    Reveal that which is hidden to my sight,
    Before darkness falls on full moon night.
    So mote it be.

- Now say this incantation out loud seven times before placing the spell paper beneath the angel statue on your altar.
- Place the tea-light in its holder before the angel. Light the wick and allow the tea-light to burn down naturally.

This spell should take effect by the full moon. As with any spell cast to reveal the truth or to bring hidden issues out into the open, there is always the risk that you will discover something that hurts your feelings, for instance a betrayal of trust or some kind of deception. While this might prove painful in the short term, in the long term it is usually better to know about such things so that you can begin to heal and restore personal balance. Then you can move on in your life. As this is an angel spell, the truth will be revealed in as gentle a way as possible.

Moving on

So far, we have explored basic angel healing rituals, covering a range of general issues. Remember that you can adapt or fine tune any of these rituals to suit your personal circumstances.

In the next chapter we will be looking at the darker aspects of life, when depression, disease and bereavement or other negative factors bring with them a dark cloud that hangs over your daily existence. On days such as these you need all the help you can get. You need the Gothic angels to help you through the dark nights of sorrow.

Dark wings

When days are dark and nights are long,
Your laughter is silenced with a mournful song.
When shadows engulf you, life has ceased to be kind,
Black bats of despair prey on your mind.
Through fog and through mist, through twilight dim,
Sorrow's bell tolls darkness in.
When Saturn lies heavy and fills your heart with his woe,
Dawn is elusive through dark nights of the soul.
When you can't clear the cobwebs from tear-filled eyes,
When faith and hope are the cruellest of lies.
Though depression is a shade through which you can't see,
Dark angels are coming to set you free...
With their dark tresses flying, their sickles that gleam,
On raven-black wings they descend through your dreams.
They cut through the shackles and the chains that bind.
They sweep away sadness giving peace to your mind.
They kiss away tears, fold you into their wings,
And into your heart a Gothic angel sings.
Your fear is now vanquished and hope is reborn,
No more do you cry or feel forlorn.
Slowly but surely, one day at a time,
They lead you through darkness 'til you feel the sun shine.
Now despair is behind you, heartbroken no more,
Dark angels have healed you through to your core.

Dark Days and Gothic Angels

We all experience the dark side of life on occasion and it is at such times that we can call on the aid of the dark angels. These angels are drawn to sadness, despair, depression, death, disease, bereavement and so on, and for this reason I refer to them as the Gothic angels. Their presence can usually be felt when there is a dark shadow hanging over your life, and only if you embrace this shadow and deal with the issue can these angels help you to move forward into the light.

The job of the Gothic angels, as with all celestial beings, is to heal. They teach us that time is the most powerful, universal healer of all afflictions and that there are usually personal lessons to be learnt during the darker days of life. These lessons will strengthen you, leaving you more ready to face whatever challenges the future holds in store. The Gothic angels can help you to absorb the teaching of such lessons more easily. If, for example, you are caught in a negative cycle of behaviour, say an addiction of some sort, then it could be that in repeating the same pattern you are closing yourself off from the lesson you need to learn. Opening up to the Gothic angels can help you to find the wisdom of this particular life lesson and so break the negative pattern.

Shadows and darkness

Attuning with the Gothic angels and working with them in ritual can help you to accept the darker aspects of nature and the shadow side of your own psyche. By this, I mean that you will come to see the usefulness and beauty of winter and night-time, you will learn to unlock the wisdom of nightmares, see the sweet release in death and find greater strength in illness and personal life challenges.

Darkness and shadows are not synonymous with evil, and working with the Gothic angels to embrace the shadow side of life should in no way be confused with the left-hand path and black magick. The darkness that we work with in witchcraft and angel craft is simply another expression of nature.

Accepting the shadow side of your psyche means accepting yourself for who you are, faults and all. We must accept our faults before we can begin working to correct them. Your shadow self is the part of you that envies others, who is jealous of a lover chatting to someone else, who is petty and vindictive. If you allow your shadow self to take complete control, you may indulge in activities you know to be wrong. While the shadow of your psyche must be accepted – after all, no one is perfect – it should not be allowed to run amok! Once again, the Gothic angels can help you to find and maintain this delicate balance.

Who are the Gothic angels?

In many books on the subject of angels, the dark angels or Gothic angels are sadly neglected and overlooked. Perhaps this is because humankind has a tendency to hide away from all aspects of darkness and the shadow side of life. Most people tend to avoid issues such as depression or addiction; they may try to deny illness and disease; they may be fearful of death. When darkness falls, they draw the curtains to shut out the velvet blackness of the night and instead turn on all the lights.

Society as a whole is conditioned to behave this way, and this negative and fearful viewpoint is reinforced on a regular basis – the elderly are treated with less respect; the ill are taken into hospices to end their days. In short, we shun that which we fear.

Prisons, drug rehabilitation centres, hospitals, nursing homes for the elderly and mentally ill, cemeteries and so on are all places that we quite naturally avoid. It is usually only when a change in circumstances forces people into one of these environments, that they become faced with this darker aspect of existence. While most people readily accept all that is light, healthy and good in the world, they tend to brush away anything that makes them feel uncomfortable or that serves to remind them of their own mortality.

This general denial of the shadow side of nature is the greatest cause of unbalance in any individual's life, and it is the role of the Gothic angels to restore this balance. The universe is based on equal polarity. In order for there to be light, there must be darkness too; for each day there is a night; for every summer a winter; for each babe born, there is also a death.

This polarity can also be seen within our own lives. To experience joy, there is usually some disappointment beforehand; to achieve success you must work your way through some failures; to appreciate true love, someone must break your heart. This is how the shadow of nature usually manifests in our lives. But the darkness and the Gothic angels are not evil. Too many people assume that anything even vaguely Gothic must be evil and therefore bad news, and in fact nothing could be further from the truth. Gothic angels are not evil and they have certainly not fallen from grace. They are celestial beings of love and healing, just like any other angel, and their role is to guide and help us through life's darkest shadows, out into the light.

I personally believe that all things Gothic, from famous novels, paintings and architecture to movies and fashion, may well have been inspired on some level by the Gothic angels. Dark angels do exist, but their sole purpose is to heal and to teach, not to harm or scare us. They only want us to accept the darkness without judgement and without fear. As the universe is divided into a polarity of light and dark, it makes perfect sense to me that the angelic dimensions are similarly divided.

What do Gothic angels look like?

As with any of the celestial beings and elementals, the Gothic angels are open to personal interpretation. It may be that you choose to visualise them as dark shadowy shapes, or in the form of smoke or mist. You may be more traditional, and visualise the Gothic angels in a more romantic way; look to the paintings and buildings of the 18th and 19th centuries for inspiration. Images of dark angels can be found carved into the stonework of Gothic architecture of the 12th–16th centuries, and such images may inspire your own imagination and visualisations. Study the works of William Blake, who was greatly inspired by the angelic realms.

In my own visualisations, I see the Gothic angels as being extremely tall, with violet eyes and long, black hair. I envision them wearing dark robes of smoky grey, silver, black, pewter and the deeper shades of purple, mulberry and maroon. They have raven black wings, and I see them flying into the circle on clouds of thunder, rain, fog and mist. I always visualise these angels carrying scythes, sickles or swords, with which they can cut away any negativity that binds us and so release us from our self-made prisons of doubt, despair and depression. They can also protect us with these weapons when we are feeling particularly vulnerable, for example when we are dealing with death or some kind of grief.

The scythe, sickle and sword are all weapons that are associated with paganism. Both the scythe and the sickle have curved blades, which symbolise the crescent moon and therefore the goddess. The sword is linked with the element of fire and is known as the sword of power, being used to cast the sacred circle and to direct energy. In visualising a Gothic angel with one of these blades, you are merging the ancient traditions of angel lore and witchcraft, and calling on the protection of both the goddess and the celestial beings.

Ritual to invoke the Gothic angels

Purpose of ritual: To ask the Gothic angels to assist you.

Items required: Your Book of Enlightenment, a pen.

Lunar phase: Any.

◆ Prepare for the ritual in the usual way (see pages 60–1).

◆ Close your eyes and bring to mind your personal image of a Gothic angel. This image should be appealing to you, and should make you feel safe and protected. Make sure your angel holds a weapon of the type described on page 88 with which to cut away anything in your life that no longer serves you or is holding you back.

◆ It may be that a name for your Gothic angel suddenly pops into your head. If so, write it down in your Book of Enlightenment, and call on your dark angel by name whenever you need his help.

◆ When you can see your dark angel clearly, say the following incantation:

On dark wings descending,
Shadows transcending,
My Gothic angel comes to me.
Sweeping away
The dark of my day,
Come dark angel and set me free!

◆ When you feel the presence of your dark angel, ask him for his assistance with your particular issue, and that he guide you through the shadows into the lighter, brighter, happier days beyond.

◆ Spend time in circle, meditating and attuning with the Gothic angels and working any spells in this chapter you choose, then blow out the candles, clear away and go about your day.

Why bad things happen to good people

If angels are all around us, all the time, why do bad things continue to happen in the world? As I explained earlier, the angels are privy to the bigger picture and they can see the greater tapestry of life. This means that while we might not be able to see the reason for something, the angels can, because they hold the secrets of the universe.

While to us, famine and war may seem to be a senseless waste of life, in some way beyond our current comprehension, these things may have a part to play. The fact that such tragedies continue to happen may indicate that humanity as a whole is just not absorbing the greater wisdom that these lessons are meant to teach us. Until we understand the true value of human life, and accept religious and cultural diversity as a great gift, war will continue to break out. Until we accept the earth and the universe as a place of natural abundance, until we learn to share and to give freely with no expectation of reward or fear of loss, famine will continue to devastate world society.

And when global tragedies do happen, the angels are very active indeed, increasing world communication, compassion and healing, lending their energies to rescue teams and aid workers, and generally inspiring people to act upon the message that help is needed *now!*

Some people seem to endure great personal tragedy and suffering in their lives, whether this be a series of accidents, contracting a serious illness or disease, or losing a loved one. While living through such circumstances can be a harrowing and trying experience, there is a certain amount of truth to the saying 'That which doesn't kill you only makes you stronger'.

Some schools of thought believe that we actively choose all the challenges we will face in life before we are born. In this way, we are active participants in our own spiritual growth. The problem is that we don't remember making these choices and so, naturally, when the challenges come along, we rebel against them. In rebelling, we close ourselves off to the wisdom of the lesson, and so leave ourselves vulnerable to repeating the same pattern.

If you accept this line of thinking, however, it suddenly becomes clear that you will never have to face anything that you cannot deal with and you will never be presented with a challenge that you cannot overcome. Just as the hero of a computer game gains points as he or she moves successfully through the levels of the game, so do you gain in strength as you move through the challenges in the game of life. And in certain situations, a negative experience can serve as a universal kick up the backside! By this I mean that if you have been living in a state of weakness and not taking responsibility for yourself or your actions, the universal law may activate a challenge on your life path, forcing you to reassess your life, your goals and your current attitude.

So, in the bigger picture, bad experiences, challenges and illness can be of benefit to you if they force you to tap into your inner strength and personal power. It may not feel that great at the time you are living through it, but in hindsight, you will probably come to see that you are stronger because of the experience and so more capable as you move on through the rest of your life.

The valley of the shadow

Death is the only certainty in life and when people are newly bereaved they sometimes turn to the angels for help and understanding. Having spent some years working in a nursing home for the elderly and having lost three members of my immediate family, I am probably better acquainted with the scythe-wielding reaper than some. While it is true that I will never actually welcome him, I have learnt to accept his presence and move through the shadow he brings one day at a time, with the healing aid of the angels.

As a society, we tend to avoid the issue of death. This effectively means that when we lose a loved one, we are forced to deal with an issue that society conditions us to repress. This makes bereavement something of a double whammy, and it can be a huge shock to the system, to say the least. For not only do you have to deal with the fact that your loved one has passed on, but you must also deal with the issue of death itself and all the ritualistic traditions that it presents. In the UK, funeral rites have changed little since the time of the Victorians, and this can add to the sense of unreality that surrounds the newly bereaved. And all this usually has to be absorbed and dealt with in the space of between five and seven days. It is hardly surprising that most people retreat into a protective shell of icy numbness, putting on a brave face and only allowing themselves to feel their loss once the public side of death is over and done with.

The grieving process itself can serve as a form of protection, allowing you to move through all the emotions associated with bereavement at your own pace. While an in-depth description of the grieving process is beyond the scope of this book, it is helpful to identify the basic stages.

Denial is the first stage of the process, in which the mind is given time to absorb the initial news. Next comes blame and guilt, when people question whose fault it is that their loved one was taken and ask themselves what they could have done to prevent the death. It is during this stage that the bereaved may become irrational and angry – usually with all the wrong people. They may be feeling anger towards the deceased for leaving them, but they often project this emotion on to doctors, friends and family members. Eventually, they move into a state of acceptance and this is when the true loss hits them and they begin to really grieve for their loved one.

Only by passing through these stages can those who are left behind begin to move on with their lives. And there is no set time limit for the grieving process to take place, so while one person may move through all the stages in just a few weeks, others may take months or even years. Understanding the stages of grief can help people to come to terms with their loss more gently and it can be of use too in comprehending the behaviour of someone who has recently been bereaved. Meditating and working angel magick can also be of help.

Celtic boat spell to come to terms with grief

Purpose of ritual: To help the bereaved deal with their loss.

Items required: Sheet of notepaper and pen; selection of small flowers, petals and blossom; Celtic cross pendant.

Lunar phase: Full to waning moon.

The nature of the universe teaches us that all things must pass, and that includes the depth of pain suffered by the recently bereaved. Time really is a great healer, and while no spell in the world can ease all of your pain, this little ritual may help you to come to terms with your loss as the Gothic angels help you begin to let go of your grief.

◆ Make all the usual ritual preparations (see pages 60–1).

◆ Settle down at your altar and think of your loved one and the time you shared together.

◆ Now put all your thoughts and emotions into words and write a letter to your deceased loved one. Allow all your emotions to flow freely on to the page.

◆ Once you have finished, fold the letter into a paper boat. Fill the boat with flowers, petals and blossom as an offering to your loved one and to the powers that be.

◆ Next to the boat, place a Celtic cross pendant. This equal-armed cross surrounded by a circle represents the four elements and the four directions joined by the circle of spirit. It symbolises both a coming together and a parting of the ways and it can serve as a reminder that all things are connected.

◆ Hold your palms down over the boat and cross and say:

Blessed be this spirit boat
And symbol of the parting ways.
Gothic angels, take these words
To one who is free of earthly days.
Gothic angels, bless this cross
And help me come to terms with loss.
So mote it be.

◆ Leave the items in place overnight, but clear away the rest of your things, and take down the circle.

◆ The following day, wear the Celtic cross as a reminder of your
connection to your loved one, and take the spell boat and flowers
to a body of tidal water.

◆ Release the boat on the out-going tide and say:

> *Gothic angels, gather here,*
> *Carry this spell to my loved one dear.*
> *Spirit to spirit, still bound as one,*
> *With angel love I now move on.*
> *Blessed be.*

Remember that your loved one will never cease to care for you as
love transcends all boundaries, including that of death. Take one day
at a time, cry when you need to and try to move forward in your life.
Go at your own pace and start to rebuild your life. Blessed be.

Spell to release a soul

Purpose of ritual: To help to release a soul from its earthly body.

Items required: Black or white candle, lighter or matches, stick of
Night Queen incense.

Lunar phase: Any.

This spell calls on the Gothic angel of death in a very positive and
gentle way. Sometimes a little magick can help to release a soul from
its earthly body, and this ritual will help to release a loved one who
is on the point of death. It is not a way of playing god or goddess,
but can serve to open the veil between the worlds, making the final
struggle easier. It can be worked for humans or pets, and should be
performed in love and trust, as with all other aspects of spell craft.
You do not need to be at your altar to perform the spell, and it can
be used whenever you feel your loved one needs it most; try to wait
until nightfall if possible.

◆ Light the candle and speak the following words:

> *If it is for the highest good of ---- (state your loved one's name),*
> *let his/her soul return to the cosmos and help me and mine to*
> *bear the loss.*

◆ Light the stick of Night Queen incense and say the following incantation, visualising a very gentle, fearless and peaceful end for your loved one as you speak:

Angel of death, I light this spark,
To summon you here through the dark.
Ease the pain and ease the flight,
Take this soul on beams of light.
By flame and smoke, this plea I send,
May magick and love bring a gentle end.
Take this soul to a better place,
Spirit fly, spirit race.
Angel of dark, angel of shadow,
Bring release and ease the sorrow.
So mote it be. Blessed be.

◆ Allow the candle to burn down naturally.

Remember that death is not the end, just another state of existence, and move forward into the light of your own life.

Coping with illness

Suffering from a serious illness or debilitating disease can have a devastating effect on your life, your mental well-being and the lives of your loved ones. Caring for someone who is ill over a long period of time can also be damaging to your health and well-being and can lead to power struggles between patient and carer. This is especially so if the invalid and carer are related. Both situations bring about their own challenges and so I will deal with each separately.

Sick and tired

When someone is initially diagnosed with a serious illness, the first response is usually 'Why me? What did I do to deserve this?' Such a reaction is completely natural as is the anger and frustration that sometimes follows. I feel, however, that it is important not to confuse illness with some kind of karmic punishment. Rather, it is just another life lesson and it will serve to increase your inner strength if you let it. Of course, this is much easier said than done. When the body is sick, it can be very difficult to keep the mind positively focused and even more of a challenge to find any level of spiritual growth within the dark realms of illness. This could be the opportunity, however, to learn to appreciate your loved ones more – and for them to appreciate you more too.

In some cases, a brief illness is the universe's way of forcing people to slow down and take things easy for a while; a few weeks nursing a broken leg could be just the 'break' you need in order to offset a more serious breakdown or illness several months down the line. Perhaps your period of illness serves as a wake-up call to somebody else, someone who relied on you quite heavily and now realises that it is time for them to stand on their own two feet. Maybe the wake-up call is for you, and the illness you are suffering is a message to alter your current lifestyle in some way. Though sickness is not a particularly pleasant experience, there is always a greater life lesson to be learnt from it.

Spell to find wisdom and strength during illness

Purpose of ritual: To help you cope with a period of illness.

Items required: Black candle, inscribing tool, lavender essential oil, dried lavender, mortar and pestle, kitchen roll, candle holder, altar pentacle.

Lunar phase: Full moon.

◆ Go to your angelic altar and make all the usual preparations (see pages 60–1).

◆ Sit quietly for a while and visualise a beautiful Gothic angel.

◆ Take the black candle and carve the words 'Gothic angels' into the wax. If you have a specific name for your Gothic angel, then carve this into the wax instead. Your candle now represents the realm of the dark angels and their magickal energies.

◆ Anoint the candle all over with lavender oil, then grind up the dried lavender using the mortar and pestle (lavender is a healing herb). Tip the dried lavender on to the kitchen roll and roll the candle through the ground flowers.

◆ Now place the candle in a holder and put the holder in the middle of the altar pentacle in the centre of the altar.

◆ Chant the following incantation seven times:

I summon dark angels here today
To take this illness far away.
Teach me the wisdom and give me strength,
I call Gothic angels their powers to lend.
By all that is high and all that is low,
Through this challenge I thrive and grow.
By the free will of all and with harm to none.
By angel love this spell is done.
So mote it be.

◆ Light the candle and allow it to burn down naturally.

◆ Remain in the sacred circle and attune with the Gothic angels for as long as you wish, then clear away your things.

Repeat the spell as often as you need to throughout the illness.

Caring for someone

Caring for a loved one is an admirable and rewarding act of service and self-sacrifice. It is probably one of the greatest expressions of love and respect you can offer someone. At the same time, it can also be exhausting and frustrating. Caring for someone with a long-term illness can be incredibly draining and it might sometimes feel as if your own life is being held to ransom and you have no time to yourself at all.

In addition, your loved one may find it difficult to accept that their independence has been compromised due to the illness and that they may not be able to do all the things they used to do for themselves. This can sometimes lead to resentment on both sides, with the invalid occasionally playing the guilt card and both parties enduring an on-going battle for control.

It is important therefore that the carer remembers to take care of him or herself too – you are no help to your loved one if you are an exhausted and emotional mess. So, accept all the help that is offered and do something that is just for you at least once a week. Go to the cinema, go dancing, go horse-riding or take a trip to the theatre. Everyone deserves a day off, including carers, who tend to be forgotten, unsung heroes. In the meantime, try the spell on the next page.

Spell for endurance and self-love

Purpose of ritual: To help a carer cope.

Items required: Two power bracelets, one of rose quartz, the other smoky quartz (alternatively use a couple of tumble stones).

Lunar phase: Full moon.

This simple spell should help to empower you as you go about your life as a carer.

◆ Place the bracelets on a windowsill in the light of the full moon and leave them there for three days and nights. Smoky quartz is associated with neutralising negativity and can help you to endure the various responsibilities of your life, while rose quartz is linked with peace and self-love and so it should remind you to take care of yourself.

◆ Once the bracelets are fully charged with full-moon energy, put them on and wear them daily.

◆ Re-charge the bracelets every full moon in exactly the same way.

◆ If you feel you need an extra power boost, call on the angels with this incantation:

Angels who see all I do,
Who know what I am going through,
Help me remain strong and true,
And let compassion reign.
Blessed be.

Spell to ease depression and despair

Purpose of ritual: To ask for the angels' help when you are feeling down.

Items required: Candles and incense (if you wish).

Lunar phase: Any.

Everyone gets a little down on occasion, but if you are having difficulty bouncing back, ask the angels to help you by using this simple pagan prayer.

◆ Light candles and incense if you wish, but this is not essential.

◆ Close your eyes and breathe deeply until you feel centred.
◆ Visualise a Gothic angel coming to free you from depression and say:

> *Guide me through shadow to sunlight bright,*
> *Guide me through darkness into the light.*
> *Bring peace to my mind,*
> *New hope let me find,*
> *Lead me through sorrow and strengthen my might.*
> *So mote it be.*

Repeat this little prayer whenever and as often as you need to.

Spell to overcome an addiction

Purpose of ritual: To strengthen will power and banish addictions.

Items required: Silver pen, black card, scissors, empty jar with a lid, several sharp objects (such as nails, pins, broken glass), glue (of the type that can be poured).

Lunar phase: Waning to dark moon.

Accepting that you have an addiction can often be the most difficult step to take, but only by accepting that you have a problem will you be able to fight it. This spell is designed to be used in conjunction with professional treatments and assistance to overcome your problem. It is not a quick fix and you must be completely committed to being free of your addiction for the spell to be effective. Remember that magick and the angels best help those who help themselves.

◆ Prepare in the usual way (see pages 60–1) and settle down at your altar.
◆ Keep in mind the positive effect being free of your addiction will have on your life, your work, your family and so on.
◆ Draw a basic angel shape on the black card and cut it out, making sure it fits into the jar.
◆ In the middle of the angel, write the nature of your addiction, for example, alcohol or cigarettes.

◆ Put the angel into the jar and add the sharp objects
  each time saying:

  Wound me no more.

◆ Now pour glue into the jar, over the sharp objects and ﹍ﹶ angel.
  As the glue sets it will help to bind the addiction.

◆ Place the lid on the jar and say:

  Gothic angels, set me free,
  Take this addiction away from me,
  Give me strength to overcome,
  By my will it shall be done.
  Remove the craving from my core,
  Let me be an addict no more.
  So mote it be.

◆ Leave the spell jar on your altar, towards the back and preferably
  behind an angel figure. Continue to attend your regular meetings
  and treatments.

If you do fall off the wagon, repeat the whole spell using the same
jar and so adding to the magick you have already made. Good luck!

Following the feathers

Now that we have dealt with the darker aspects of life, it is time for
the Gothic angels to lead you forward into the light so that you can
replace the negatives you have released in this chapter with positive
things instead. We begin with the angel of love and beauty,
Archangel Gabriel and her winged steeds.

Gabriel and her steed

Across the lake, through silvery mist,
Gabriel rides in from the west.
As twilight falls early and darkness descends,
Through enchanted forest her way she wends.
Seated upon a white faerie-steed,
The pair make their way through bracken and reed,
With a bridle of gossamer and harness of gold,
Both horse and angel have wings to unfold.
With horseshoes of silver that ring in the rain,
Autumn-gold leaves fashion Gabriel's train.
Her steed dips his head to drink from the lake
And the silk of his mane and tail he shakes.
The wind whispers softly as Gabriel sings,
Then her steed stamps his hooves and spreads out his wings.
With a neigh and a song they take to the sky
And scatter white feathers for children to find.
So fast do they fly, Gabriel and her steed,
As they gallop their way into your dreams.

Angels of Love and Passion

Our relationships are an intrinsic part of our lives and they go a long way in contributing to our well-being and overall happiness. The bonds we form with friends, parents, family members and romantic partners help to shape our lives and, to a certain extent, our personalities too.

If you are happy in your close relationships and enjoy a stable home life, then you have a firm foundation from which you can face various life challenges. A strong support system, or lack of one, can be a fundamental factor in the success or failure of any one individual. It is much easier to strive for success and overcome problems when the people you love encourage you and spur you on to succeed. If your loved ones have a more negative viewpoint however, they may offer only negative criticism or try to undermine your confidence in general. It can be tough to be told at every turn that you will never make anything of yourself, and in such a situation it can seem as if the people you love most in the world only want to see you fail. On the other hand, this type of negative feedback can be just the thing to spur you on and make you determined to succeed, if only to prove them wrong.

I have some experience of this myself. When I was struggling to become a published writer, someone close to me suggested that I would do better to get a steady job in a supermarket, rather than pursuing my dream, as I'd never make it as an author. The publication of my first book was also described as nothing more than 'a flash in the pan'. At the time I found these negative opinions and remarks to be very hurtful but now, nine books and two publishers later, I do feel as if I have proved these particular people wrong and that I have had the last laugh.

So do try to keep in mind that while negative feedback of any sort from your loved ones can be difficult to hear, it won't necessarily sabotage your ambitions and ultimate success. Having said that, success with a positive support system is probably much sweeter.

Relationships can also have an effect on other aspects of your life. One common complaint is that when people fall in love they inadvertently begin to neglect their relationships with family, colleagues and friends in favour of spending more time with the new love interest or spouse. And, if someone is in the process of falling out of love, going through a bitter break-up or divorce or just experiencing a few marital difficulties, the upset and mental strain of this can have a negative effect on their health, their performance at work and so on.

Withholding love

One of the most common failings of human beings is that we tend to use love as a weapon or bargaining tool. By this, I mean that, on occasion, we forget to live the truth of unconditional love. By withholding affection, communication, approval and support from a loved one, we are attempting to manipulate and exercise control over that person. While such behaviour may be entirely unconscious, it can still be extremely damaging to the relationship and to the individuals involved. This type of conditional love and controlling behaviour stems from fear and insecurity, and it says far more about the person trying to exercise control than it does about their loved one.

If we make a conscious effort to communicate from a place of unconditional love, while maintaining respect for a loved one's independence, unique personality and individual life path, then it becomes much harder to manipulate that person inadvertently. In the long term, this makes for a healthy, stable relationship that is based on trust.

It is essential that you are as happy as you can be in all your close personal relationships and that you work continuously towards maintaining positive lines of communication with your loved ones. Working magickally with the angels and inviting these beings of love into your life can help you to improve your communications with people and can have a very positive effect on all your relationships. And perhaps more importantly, the angels can teach us about the true beauty and value of unconditional love.

Last of the great romantics

When people think of love they often think of romance, and the two do seem to complement one another exceptionally well. If you are lucky, you will experience both love and romance at the same time with the same person – though there are no guarantees!

I have always been an incurable romantic and I make no apologies for this. My life is filled with romance, from the clothes I wear, the poetry and novels I read, the music I listen to, the paintings hung on my walls and the way in which I have decorated my home. I firmly believe in true love's first kiss, but while I may have my fair share of 'princess issues' to deal with, I do not believe that my independence and personality should be compromised for the sake of enjoying a little romance.

Romance is wonderful, but our expectations of love and relationships must be grounded in reality. Otherwise, we run the risk of being eternally disappointed. However much you may like to dream of the perfect knight in shining armour, however much you may wish that Lancelot would ride up on a white charger and rescue you from a life of monotony, the sad fact is that knights don't exist anymore – though leather-clad bikers come pretty close. By the same token, although a man may dream of the perfect supermodel, he is more likely to find lasting happiness with a real woman, flaws and all.

So, rather than waiting for the perfect knight to come along, be proactive and get out there, meeting new people. As you do so, try to see the chivalry in *all* men. One trick I found useful when working in bars and clubs was to appeal to a man's inner knight – by this I mean that you should expect a man to show the better side of his nature. When we expect the best of people, that is usually what we get, as our expectations become our reality. The same is true, of course, for men who want to meet their romantic ideal.

Being overly romantic though could lead to unrealistic ideas of what a relationship should be. All lovers have their spats and disagreements and no couple spends their entire relationship cooing at one another like a pair of doves. A relationship is romance with a reality twist in the tale.

If you are single or feel that romance is lacking in your life, there are many other ways to experience the essence of romance without the need for a relationship or partner. Seek the romance you are after in books, films, poetry and artwork. Visit romantic places, such as Paris, buy yourself red roses and chocolates. This is a great way to open yourself up to the possibility of love and romance if you are single and looking for that special someone to share your romantic sentiments with. Enjoy and express your romantic tendencies, but do not allow yourself to be totally governed by them – try to maintain a firm grip on reality.

Ethics of love magick

Because relationships involve someone else as well as yourself, love spells and magick of a romantic nature are governed by a strict code of ethics. This goes back to the issue of free will (see page 12).

The main rule of love magick is that you should never cast a spell on a specific person or with a particular individual in mind. In doing so, you would be interfering in that person's free will and freedom of choice. This goes against all the ethics of positive magick and the Wiccan rede, which states that you should 'harm none'.

In general, love spells are cast with an image of our ideal love in mind, and while focusing on specific qualities such as kindness, honesty and faithfulness, rather than visualising or naming a specific individual. In this way, love magick brings the person that is right for you at that particular point in your life. Occasionally, infatuations can lead you in totally the wrong direction. While you might think that Mr Whoever is the right man for you, he could prove to be everything you never wanted.

You should never use love spells to try to steal someone away from his or her partner. The threefold law states that whatever you send out, whether good or bad, you will get back with three times the force. So if you use a spell in this way, you are sure to pay for it in the end. Keep your love magick general and you are likely to be pleasantly surprised by the results.

What about magick cast to improve other relationships? Spells can be cast to help marital, parental, sibling and career relationships, as well as close personal friendships. Again, the magick should be cast to bring improvements to the relationship, rather than to try to change an individual. Magick can also be used to change your own attitude to a relationship and how you react to confrontation within the dynamics of that relationship. This often proves to be the most effective method as the only person we can truly change is ourselves.

Archangel Gabriel

Archangel Gabriel is probably the best known of all the archangels. Ask a child to name an angel and Gabriel is likely to be top of the list. This is largely due to Gabriel's role in the Bible as the messenger who told Mary she was expecting baby Jesus. No school nativity play would be complete without Archangel Gabriel being represented, feathered wings and all.

Although some people prefer to think of Gabriel as masculine, I have always perceived the energies of this angel to be feminine and view her as the glamorous superstar of the celestial realms. In magickal terms, Gabriel is associated with the element of water, so if you were born into the astrological sign of Scorpio, Cancer or Pisces then you will have a natural affinity with Gabriel and she is already guiding you on your life path and watching over you.

Gabriel is associated with the direction of west and the magickal hour of dusk. Autumn is her season with the autumnal equinox being her sacred time, so visualise her in robes of soft golds, bronze, russet, dark stormy blue and, of course, white, which is the colour of all angels.

Gabriel is linked with the moon and her sacred animal is the horse, especially white and palomino horses. She is also linked with the equines of mythology such as the beautiful unicorn and the magnificent winged horse. I tend to visualise Gabriel riding one of these magickal beasts, particularly the winged horse and I felt inspired to write the opening poem for this chapter after meditating on such a vision.

Archangel Gabriel is the foremost among the divine messengers. She is a great protector of women and children, and she understands the nature of girl power and feminine wisdom and empowerment. She has a beautiful romantic essence, and can enable you to improve all your relationships, by helping you to both feel and share the love more easily. She can teach you how to nurture yourself and increase your sense of self-love. Working magickally with Archangel Gabriel can guide you towards finding that special someone. Visualise her riding a white winged horse, swathed in a cloak of autumn-gold leaves and carrying a pure white rose, which symbolises her gift of unconditional love.

Ritual to evoke your inner goddess

Purpose of ritual: To call on your inner goddess or god.

Items required: Candles, incense (optional).

Lunar phase: Any.

All human beings hold a spark of divinity within them. Men have a spark of the god-force, while we women each have our own inner goddess. As angels are the link between humankind and the divine, it stands to reason that they can help us to get in touch with our own inner divinity. Archangel Gabriel can help women to attune with their inner goddess and to realise the full potential of their power. For men, the angel to call on to free the inner god-force would be Archangel Michael, and male readers can simply substitute the name in the incantation below.

◆ First of all, take a long ritual bath and dress in your magickal robes or a loose-fitting nightgown.

◆ Go to your angelic altar and prepare in the usual way (see pages 60–1). Light the candles and some incense if you wish to.

◆ Sit quietly for a while and think of all that is wonderful about womanhood and feminine power. Feel your power as a woman and remember all the life challenges that you have overcome.

◆ When you are ready, call on Archangel Gabriel in the following way:

Angel Gabriel, hear this plea,
Help me to find the goddess in me.
My sacred power I would see,
My inner goddess can set me free.

◆ Remain at your altar and quietly contemplate where your life is going and how you wish to use your goddess power in the future. Know that Gabriel has heard your prayer and that she will assist you from now on.

Whenever you need to summon your goddess strength, simply call on Gabriel and repeat the incantation above.

Spell for unconditional love

Purpose of ritual: To encourage unconditional love.

Items required: Bunch of white roses or lilies.

Lunar phase: New to full moon.

Sometimes it may feel as if a loved one is putting conditions on their affection for you, or vice versa. If someone you love gets stroppy because you have been busy with other aspects of your life, or if they threaten to leave you in order to make you do or not do something, then that is conditional love. We are all guilty of this on occasion but if it becomes a frequent problem, try working this spell to encourage unconditional love on both sides of the relationship.

◆ Start by preparing a ritual bath. Place the roses or lilies on your altar, and taking a single flower from the bunch, scatter its petals into the bath water.

◆ As you soak, imagine that you are soaking up unconditional love and that your loved one's attempts at manipulation will have no effect on you whatsoever.

◆ After your bath, prepare for ritual in the usual way (see pages 60–1).

◆ Hold the bunch of flowers up at the western quarter of the circle, offering them to Gabriel, and say:

I offer these roses to Gabriel that she may bless them with her gift of unconditional love. When I give these roses to ---- let the manipulation of conditional love be at an end. So mote it be.

◆ Leave one flower on your altar in offering to Gabriel and give the rest to your loved one to seal the spell. You should notice a difference within seven days.

Old habits die hard, so perform the spell whenever you feel the need.

Spell to attract a new love

Purpose of ritual: To pull a new love into your life.

Items required: Your favourite incense, pen and paper, altar pentacle, angel statue, cauldron or heatproof dish.

Lunar phase: Full moon.

◆ Prepare for ritual in the usual way (see pages 60–1).

◆ Once you are settled at your angelic altar, light a stick of your favourite incense. Focus on the smoke travelling upwards to the celestial realms, and begin to think about what you want in a romantic relationship.

◆ Now write a letter to Gabriel, asking that she bring your ideal partner into your life. Describe the qualities of this person and be as detailed as you can without actually naming or focusing on any one individual. Sign and date the letter, and then write three more copies of the same letter.

◆ Fold one letter and place it on your altar pentacle with the angel statue on top. Place the second copy beneath your pillow or under your bed. Burn the third copy in the cauldron and keep the fourth copy in your bag or wallet so that you have the spell with you in your daily life.

Now keep your eyes peeled for your ideal love. A spell like this one can take between six months and a year to manifest, so don't worry if nothing seems to happen straight away. Repeat the spell in six months' time, and keep the faith.

Spell to increase romance

Purpose of ritual: To bring the essence of romance into your life.

Items required: Small statue of a loving couple, box of chocolates, bottle of wine, selection of items that suggest romance to you (for example, romantic pictures, films, poetry).

Lunar phase: New to full moon.

Whether married or divorced, attached or single, sometimes we all need a little extra romance in our lives. Instead of waiting for the man of the moment to provide it for you, kick-start the romance yourself. As the angel of love and romance, Gabriel can guide you in transforming your living space into a romantic haven.

◆ First of all you need to go shopping for the statue, chocolates, wine and selection of items that suggest the essence of romance to you. You needn't spend a fortune. Try looking in markets and country fairs for a few bargain items, or hunt around the attic and see what you find.

◆ Once you have a collection of objects, put them all in a pile and wave your wand over them seven times, saying:

> *Gabriel of angel grace,*
> *Lend romance to my living space.*
> *Fill my life with romance rare,*
> *Pure angel love I wish to share!*

◆ Now place your romantic items around your home, putting the statue of the loving couple in a prominent position. Settle down in your new romantic retreat and enjoy the wine and chocolates while watching a romantic film or reading love poetry.

Once you begin to actively put the romance into your home and surround yourself with the essence of romantic love, it should be drawn into your life.

Spell to increase passion

Purpose of ritual: To bring more passion to your relationship.

Items required: Red paper, pen, scissors, pouch, two small ivy leaves, mixed spices, small angel charm, ylang ylang oil, altar pentacle.

Lunar phase: new moon

◆ Go to your altar and prepare for ritual in the usual way (see pages 60–1).

◆ Settle down at your altar and think of your partner and the love you share. Think about putting the passion and the heat back into the relationship, or just turning things up a notch to avoid repetition.

◆ Now cut two love hearts from the red paper and write your own name on one and your partner's name on the other.

◆ Take up the pouch and place the two hearts inside saying:

My heart for you, your heart for me.

◆ Add the ivy leaves and say:

Ivy binds in fidelity.

◆ Add a small pinch of mixed spice and say:

A pinch of spice to stir the flame.

◆ Add the angel charm and say:

This spell I cast in Gabriel's name.

◆ Tie the neck of the pouch and then sprinkle it with ylang ylang oil, saying:

Raise the passion, fan the flame,
Stir the blood and call my name.
Send me spinning all around,
Our renewed passion knows no bounds.
So mote it be.

◆ Leave the pouch on your altar pentacle to charge for three nights, then place it beneath the bed or hang it from the bedpost.

Ritual to promote self-love

Purpose of ritual: To nurture yourself.

Items required: Three rose quartz crystals; altar pentacle; pink, rose-scented pillar candle with a suitable holder.

Lunar phase: Any.

In a world where most people are busy taking care of family, meeting work commitments and generally rushing around like headless chickens, it can sometimes feel as if we have forgotten to take care of ourselves. If you seem to be facing lots of criticism or if you just need a bit of a boost, then a self-love ritual can be exactly what you need to remind yourself that you are a unique and beautiful person.

This is a very simple ritual and you don't need to cast a circle or call the quarters to perform it. Just spend a little time by yourself at your angel altar, preferably in the evenings before going to bed.

◆ Place the three rose quartz crystals on the altar pentacle and place the pillar candle in its holder.

◆ Breathe deeply for a while and concentrate on releasing all the negative happenings of the day from your mind.

◆ Light the candle and place your hands either side of it, palms facing inwards. Say the following incantation:

I am light, I am bright,
I am pure, I am self-assured,
I am love, I am enough,
I am stable, I am capable,
I am wise, I see through lies.
Confidence awaken, I will not be shaken.
I am health, I am wealth.
In the name of all angels above,
I am strong in my self-love.
Blessed be.

◆ Allow the candle to burn a little and meditate on the flame until you feel calm and centred.

◆ Blow out the candle and place the rose quartz crystals as follows: one on the angelic altar, one by your bed and one in your bag or on your desk at work. These crystals will link you with the angel spell and remind you to nurture yourself throughout your day.

◆ Now relax for the rest of the evening, or go directly to bed.

Repeat the ritual each evening for the best results and you should soon be feeling confident, strong and in control.

Spell to help heal a broken heart

Purpose of ritual: To help you move on after a divorce or break-up.

Items required: Inscribing tool, white candle, pink candle, black candle, red thread, heatproof candle platter.

Lunar phase: Full moon.

It can take time to get over a romantic break-up or divorce, and you should give yourself the opportunity to accept the break before performing this angel spell. When you feel that you are ready to face the future and move forward in your life, cast this spell which utilises the energies of Archangel Gabriel and the Gothic angels.

◆ Prepare for spellcasting in the usual way (see pages 60–1) and settle down at your altar.

◆ Using your athame or an inscribing tool such as a craft or kitchen knife, inscribe your name on to the white candle. Next inscribe 'Archangel Gabriel' on to the pink candle and 'Gothic angel' on to the black candle. You now have a candle to represent the three elements of the spell: yourself, Gabriel and the Gothic angels.

◆ Hold the three candles in one hand, forming a triangle, with the white candle at the apex, and bind them tightly together using the red thread. These candles now represent the protection and support the angels give you through this challenging time in your life.

◆ Once the candles are bound securely together, stand them on the platter and light all three wicks.

◆ Focusing on the flames, begin to chant the following:
Archangel Gabriel, heal my heart.
Gothic angels, heal my heart.
May angel love heal my heart.

◆ Continue chanting for as long as you comfortably can, then allow the three candles to burn down naturally, keeping an eye on them as you go about your day. This can take some time, so make sure you have several hours free in which to work the spell.

Move on with your life at your own pace and feel the energies of the angels helping you to progress.

Spell to bring harmony to family relationships

Purpose of ritual: To create a state of harmony within your family.

Items required: Photo of your family or specific relation, white feathers, glue.

Lunar phase: New to full moon.

◆ Take all the items required to your angel altar and prepare as usual (see pages 60–1).

◆ Light the candles and incense.

◆ Sit for a while and visualise a harmonious relationship existing within your family and between all family members. Imagine your family being bathed in peace and unconditional love for one another.

◆ Now take up the photograph and begin to glue white feathers around the edge, so framing the picture in feathers. As you glue each feather in place, say:

> *White feathers surround you,*
> *By blood I am bound to you,*
> *Love all around you,*
> *May harmony surround you.*

◆ Continue until you have framed the edge of the photo in feathers. Leave the photo on your altar for seven days and nights.

You should see and feel a difference in your family dynamics and communications within a week or so. Keep the photo on or near your angel altar to keep the magick strong.

Spell to deepen the bond with friends and colleagues

Purpose of ritual: To enhance personal and professional relationships.

Items required: Tea-light and holder.

Lunar phase: New to full moon.

◆ Prepare for ritual as usual (see pages 60–1).
◆ Place the tea-light in a holder at the centre of your angelic altar.
◆ Focus on the flame and begin to chant:

I call on Gabriel, her power to lend,
To strengthen the bond with my colleagues and friends.
For the free will of all and with harm to none,
By angel love this spell is done.

◆ Repeat the chant seven times and allow the candle to burn down naturally, then go about your daily life as usual.

Gabriel's steed meditation

This guided meditation in which you visualise a journey is called a pathworking. You do not need to be at your altar, but can perform it in your bedroom or even out of doors if you prefer. You will find it much easier to concentrate on the meditative journey if you record the meditation on tape, or if you have a friend read it out to you slowly and calmly.

Begin by sitting comfortably and concentrating on your breathing. Breathe slowly and deeply until you feel calm and centred. Close your eyes and, in your mind, begin to visualise the following journey.

◆ You are walking through a thick, dark forest. It is autumn and the leaves are turning from green to shades of russet and gold. Dry twigs crack beneath your feet as you walk and you pull your forest-green cloak around you more closely to keep out the chill of the air. A pale sun is shining, filtering through the trees and casting shadows of dancing leaves upon the forest floor. It gives little warmth though and the air is damp with autumn mist.

◆ You breathe deeply as you walk, enjoying the earthy fragrance of the damp forest and feeling content as you make your way through the woods. Up ahead, a roe deer crosses your path, pausing for a moment to look at you with her huge, brown, gentle eyes, before she moves on through the forest. The birds are twittering as they return to their nests, for darkness falls early in the autumnal forest and it will soon be dusk.

◆ In the distance you can hear the sound of water and the gentle lapping of soft waves. You make your way towards the sound, following the hypnotic murmur of the water and, pushing through the tangled forest-hair of a weeping willow tree, you find yourself looking out upon a misty blue lake. A small waterfall feeds into the lake, playing over rocks and pebbles as it falls into the mass of water below. You take in the beauty of your surroundings, sitting down on a moss-covered stone to gaze out over the water.

◆ Soon you hear the sound of galloping hooves coming from the far side of the lake and, in a flash of white and gold, Gabriel and her winged steed come riding in from the west. You stand up and move closer to the water's edge as Gabriel smiles across at you, allowing her horse to drink the pure crystal water of the lake. Gabriel motions to you to join her and, looking down, you notice a trail of stepping stones just beneath the surface of the water. They weren't there a moment ago, but still you sit down to remove your footwear and step into the water. Feeling the rocks firm beneath your feet and the cool, silky water lapping at your ankles, you skip lightly over the stepping stones and, in moments, you find yourself on the western shore of the lake at Gabriel's side.

◆ 'Welcome child,' says Gabriel, as her horse raises his head from the lake to nuzzle you, dripping lake water down your shoulder. You laugh and give him a gentle pat. Then you begin to talk with Gabriel. You can ask her anything you like, so spend as long as you wish here at Gabriel's sacred lake and get to know this loving angel and her magickal steed.

◆ When you are ready, you turn to go and Gabriel plucks a white feather from one of her wings, hands it to you and says, 'Look for me in dreams. Know that I will always be with you and that you can return to me here at any time.'

◆ Gabriel's horse then nuzzles you once more in farewell and you give him a final pat before making your way back across the stepping stones to the eastern side of the lake once more.

◆ You sit to put on your shoes, gazing over at Gabriel who waves in farewell. Then with a joyful neigh, her steed rears, spreads his wings and leaps up into the mist to take to the sky. You watch them fly away, feeling blessed in the wisdom and guidance Gabriel has given you.

◆ You turn and walk back through the willow boughs; back through the forest; back to the everyday world, to your current surroundings and to the present moment in time.

Open your eyes when you are ready. You can repeat this meditational pathworking as often as you like.

Gabriel's love

This chapter offers only a small sample of what working magickally with Gabriel can do to enhance your relationships. Angel love is unlimited, it knows no bounds, so call on Gabriel's help whenever you feel you need to. Feel free to create your own relationship rituals too, using Gabriel's love and light as your main focus for the spell.

Occasionally, you may feel that you need more than gentle love from your angel friends. You may need their support as you face adversity, or strong defence from those who mean you harm – in short, you need angelic protection, and that is where the celestial warrior Archangel Michael makes his timely entrance.

Guardian angel's prayer

May your childhood be happy and your family hold true,
May your playtimes be fun, may you learn much in school,
May you grow in good health, may you always be strong,
May you live life in laughter, raise your voice in a song.
As you grow into adulthood, new challenges you'll meet,
May you find your true path laid out at your feet,
May you live life in love, may your sweetheart be true,
May you find much success in all that you do.
If you start your own family, may they bring you great joy,
May you cherish your children, both girl and boy.
And when times are tough, remember I'm here,
I will guide and protect you, help you see your way clear.
And when you lie in your bed, old now and frail,
Take hold of my hand and we'll fly through the veil.

Angels of Protection

When people think of angels they usually think of life-saving incidents and divine protection. There is no doubt in my mind that our guardian angels protect us on a daily basis, not always in a sensational way, but sometimes more subtly, for example guiding us to drive a different way into work to avoid an accident on our usual route. That inner voice that warns you to avoid a certain place or person could well be the voice of your guardian angel.

Today's world being what it is, there are likely to be times when you feel less than safe, or even downright vulnerable. Anything that makes you feel uncomfortable is worth dealing with. You are not being paranoid, you are being sensible. It is far better to be safe than sorry and if this means that you only answer the door when you are expecting someone, that you keep the doors locked and chained when you are home alone and that your house resembles Fort Knox, then so be it.

There are many things that can make you feel vulnerable and not all of them are a direct threat. Spitefulness and malicious gossip, bullying at work or place of study, a partner who has an alcohol or drug abuse problem, walking home from work late at night or after dark in winter time, being approached by a stranger, groups of youths hanging around the streets, noticing a questionable character in the park as you play with your kids: all these things and many more can put you on edge and leave you feeling unsafe.

These feelings do not mean that you are being weak, as fear is nature's way of alerting you to the fact that something is not quite right. Fear is a protection device, it gives you the time to act, whereas in a state of total panic you can only react. The trick is to become more aware of when you feel vulnerable, unsafe and afraid. As soon as you recognise these emotions in yourself, get out of that particular situation. Don't wait until the fear becomes panic, but act when you feel uncomfortable, removing yourself from the situation as calmly and quickly as possible. And to increase your feelings of safety, work protection magick regularly.

How protection magick works

Protection magick works on the basis that prevention is better than cure. By this, I mean that you should work protection magick even when you don't feel afraid and not just when you feel threatened in some way. Most magickal practitioners and witches work some form of protection magick on a daily basis. This keeps the magick strong and helps to prevent anything harmful from reaching you.

In a sense, protection magick can be likened to the defences of a castle. Think about the great medieval castles that are dotted around the UK. These castles were built to defend and protect. In order to take the castle, the invader would have to cross a town wall or a moat, or climb a cliff, negotiate their way over the drawbridge, get beyond the portcullis of the outer bailey, then get beyond the portcullis of the inner bailey and defeat the armed guard – all before they were anywhere near the keep itself. The strength of these great castles is in their layer upon layer of defences.

Protection magick works in a similar way in that the witch layers on the rituals one after another, creating a magickal web of defence. To protect her house, for example, a witch might place protective crystals at the four cardinal points of the front and back gardens, thus protecting the outer perimeter. Then she might cast a protective circle around the house itself and invoke an angel or thoughtform (a visualisation of a particular guardian) to guard the entrance. Once inside the house, she would magickally ward all the doors and windows and perhaps hang a mirrored wind chime in the front window to deflect any negativity sent her way. In this way, she layers her protection magick and so strengthens her defences. (See page 128 for household protection magick.)

Victim or survivor?

All the angels and protection magick in the world won't make you feel safe and in control if you have the wrong attitude. If you think of yourself as a victim then that is exactly what you are likely to become. The world can be a scary place at times and there are some dangerous people out there, and some people do seem to have more than their fair share of trials and challenges; but if you think and act like a victim, then you are effectively giving all your power away to the bad guys.

So, how do you know if you have developed a victim mentality? It tends to go hand in hand with the martyr mind set, so if you find yourself harping on about every bad thing that has ever happened to you, if you constantly play the 'poor little me' role, if you tell the world about all the sacrifices you have made, if you wear your broken dreams as badges of honour – then you are living the life of a victim who is at the mercy of life, and you need to do something to change your ways.

While it is true that everyone needs to have a little moan every now and then, turning this into a lifestyle choice can be very damaging to your mental health, possibly even leading to depression and feelings of desperation. It can also be the fastest way to lose friends, as people tend to distance themselves from someone who is depressed. In addition, by focusing on all the negatives in your life, you could well be attracting yet more chaos and catastrophe.

It is in your best interests to learn to think of yourself as a survivor, rather than a victim, and to get in touch with your warrior spirit. If something negative does happen in your life then by all means have a brief moan to your friends about it, but try to tell the tale with a strong injection of comedy, as finding a sense of humour in the midst of your troubles and laughing at your adversary is the best way to empower yourself and disarm your enemy. Once you have indulged in a quick gripe, try to forget about the problem and move on with your life. In this way, you will lose the victim mentality and give your warrior spirit free rein.

Archangel Michael

Michael is the great warrior of all the archangels. He is the strong right hand of the celestial realms. He is usually depicted carrying a huge sword, which he uses to defend the innocent and punish the guilty. As the angel of justice, Michael is sometimes depicted bearing the scales of justice, with which he can weigh up souls, totting up the crimes of wrong-doers and doling out karmic retributions.

As a divine protector, Michael is the heroic armoured knight of the angelic dimensions and his loyalty is legendary. Once you have made a connection with Michael, he will never leave you unprotected and he will leap to your defence a thousand times, if necessary. If you share the same name as this angel or one of the feminine derivatives such as Michelle or Michaela, then it could be that you naturally have quite heroic tendencies and you may be strongly in tune with your warrior spirit.

Michael is linked with the sun and he is associated with the season of summer. In magickal terms, he is linked with the element of fire so if you were born into one of the fire signs (Aries, Leo and Sagittarius), then you may also have a natural affinity with this angel, who is guiding you on your life path and watching over you. As you may have noticed from the quarter calls, Michael presides over the direction south. His magickal hour is noon, being the hottest part of the day, and the summer solstice is his sacred time.

Visualise Michael in pale to mid blue, the colour of the summer sky; and also in silver and white. See him flying in from the south, the sun shining brightly behind him, his feet swathed in fluffy white clouds. His blue robes billow out around him, his sword glints in the sunlight and his golden, sunlit hair shines like a halo. Meditate and connect with him at one of the many Michael's Mounts that are dotted on ley lines all over Europe, such as the one in Cornwall.

Spell to evoke your warrior spirit

Purpose of ritual: To bring out inner strength and heroic qualities.

Items required: None.

Lunar phase: Any.

We all like to think that we could be heroes if the need ever arose but perhaps the most heroic thing we will ever do is just to get through the challenges of our daily lives. If you feel that your confidence needs a boost, or that you need to be able to summon up your personal strength at the drop of a hat, then try using this spell to help you connect with your inner warrior spirit.

◆ Repeat this positive affirmation whenever you feel the need:

Michael; warrior, angel, friend,
I summon you, your strength to lend.
Raise your sword, protect, defend!
Michael, wrap your
wings around me,
Set my warrior spirit free.
I face all foes and adversity.
By angel love, so mote it be.

Commit the words to memory so that you can call on Michael at any time.

Ring-a-rose angels' protection spell

Purpose of ritual: To protect your home and property.

Items required: Two small onions, knife, large tub of rock or sea salt (or table salt if you don't have rock or sea salt), white rose petals, tealight and holder.

Lunar phase: Perform each full moon for best effect.

Earlier I explained that protection magick was similar to the layered defences of a castle. You are now going to put that theory into practice by layering the magickal defences of your own castle – that is, your home and garden (if you have one).

- This is an 'on the go' spell, which means that you will be moving around and working the spell both out of doors and indoors, and around your property, so do not cast the circle and call the quarters at your altar. Instead collect all the items you need in your kitchen and work from there.

- Cut the onions in half, giving you four pieces of onion. Place one half at each of the cardinal points of your outer space or garden (north, south, east and west), effectively marking the perimeters of your property. Magickally, onions are often used to absorb negativity and so this will help to keep your property safe from harm. If you do not have any outside space, move indoors around the perimeter of your property.

- Return to the kitchen and get the salt. Go back outside and begin to scatter a circle of salt all around the perimeter of your property, passing by each of the onions you have placed. If your home is attached to another property, pass through the house and throw a small pinch of salt along the inside adjoining wall. As you do so, chant:

Protected be.

- Now repeat the circle again, this time scattering salt around the outside of the house itself and keeping the salt as close to the walls as possible, continuing to chant as you go. You now have three layers of protection: the onions and two cast circles of salt.

◆ Finally pick up the white rose petals and scatter these in a circle directly around the outside of your house, following the line of the inner circle of salt. This time visualise a circle of angels holding hands and surrounding your home. As you scatter the petals, chant:

> *By this ring of roses,*
> *I play the angel hostess.*
> *Angels circle all around*
> *And keep my home safe and sound.*

◆ Once your ring of roses is cast, return to the house and burn the tea-light on your angelic altar to seal the spell.

Remember to keep your visualisation strong and to repeat the ritual once a month, if possible, to reinforce the protection magick.

Spell to deflect neighbourhood negativity

Purpose of ritual: To send back any negative energies directed at your home.

Items required: Wind chime that has small mirrors attached, lavender oil.

Lunar phase: Waning to dark moon.

◆ Prepare for ritual in the usual way (see pages 60–1), taking the mirrored wind chime and lavender oil to your altar with you.

◆ When you feel ready, hold your hands palms down over the wind chime and say:

> *I call on Michael in honour and respect,*
> *May these mirrors his love reflect.*
> *As all negativity they deflect,*
> *May these chimes ring in peace,*
> *May all negativity now cease.*
> *In Michael's name, this spell I release.*
> *So mote it be.*

◆ Splash the chime with a few drops of lavender oil for peace and tranquillity, then hang the chime in an upper window at the front of the house to do its work.

To enhance this spell, perform it in conjunction with the ring-a-rose angels' protection spell (see pages 128–9).

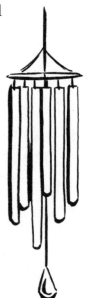

Angelic binding spell

Purpose of ritual: To bind one who would do you harm.

Items required: Slip of paper, pen, seven pins, three white feathers, glue (of the type that you can pour), jar with a lid.

Lunar phase: Waning to dark moon.

◆ Take all the items required to your altar and prepare in the usual way (see pages 60–1).

◆ Spend a few moments thinking of the person who is trying to hurt you or cause you distress, for example, the bully at work or the neighbours from hell.

◆ Write the person's name on the slip of paper, place the paper in the jar and say:

> *The hurt you cause is now at an end,*
>
> *I return to you all the negativity you send.*

◆ Add the seven pins, one by one and each time you drop a pin into the jar, say:

> *May this pin prick your conscience.*

◆ Next add the three feathers. As you add the first one say:

> *May my guardian angel protect me.*

◆ As you add the second feather, say:

> *May angel love surround me.*

◆ Add the third feather and say:

> *May Michael's sword defend me.*

◆ Pour glue into the jar and say:

> *I bind ---- (name your adversary) from doing me harm.*
>
> *By angel power, I am protected, safe and calm.*
>
> *So mote it be.*

◆ Put the lid on the jar and leave it in place on your altar.

You should notice that the person who has been troubling you leaves you alone within one lunar month. Reinforce the magick each day by holding the jar and repeating the final binding words of the spell three times.

Spell to end malicious gossip

Purpose of ritual: To stop someone talking about you in a spiteful way.

Items required: Inexpensive fashion doll, black marker pen, white feather, glue, white ribbon, shoebox with a lid, clove oil.

Lunar phase: Waning to dark moon.

◆ Take all the items to your altar and prepare as usual (see pages 60–1).

◆ When a doll is used in magick to represent a person, it is called a poppet. Sit with the poppet for a few minutes and think about the person who is gossiping about you and the things that they have been saying.

◆ Now write the name of the gossip on the torso of the poppet, using the black marker pen.

◆ Take the white feather and glue it in place over the mouth of the poppet, then bind it firmly in place with the white ribbon. As you do this, say the following incantation:

> *May Raphael heal your spite,*
> *May Michael cut the thread of your vicious thoughts and words,*
> *May Gabriel silence you,*
> *May Uriel bind your negativity.*
> *So ends your gossip and spitefulness.*
> *May angels protect me from your negativity always.*
> *So mote it be.*

◆ Place the newly bound poppet into the shoebox, sprinkle it with clove oil and say:

> *With oil of clove, I cleanse your spite,*
> *May you speak only words of truth and light.*
> *So mote it be.*

◆ Put the lid on the shoebox and hold it down with both hands as you say:

> *I cast this spell in Michael's name,*
> *To put an end to gossip's game.*
> *This spell goes forth in Michael's light,*
> *So ends all lies, so ends this spite.*

◆ Place the shoebox at the back of a dark cupboard where the poppet will not be disturbed.

Guardian angel magick

The following spells utilise the power of the angel closest to you – your personal guardian angel. Remember too that you can include your guardian angel in any of the other spells in this book, simply by asking for their assistance with the ritual.

Angel blessings ritual

Purpose of ritual: To invoke angelic protection for your loved ones.

Items required: As many guardian angel brooches as you have loved ones, plus one extra for yourself.

Lunar phase: Full moon.

◆ Allow the guardian angel pins to charge on your altar pentacle for 24 hours prior to the spell. Then prepare as usual (see pages 60–1).

◆ Hold your hands over the pins and say:

> *Guardian angels, I call you here,*
> *Please protect my loved ones dear.*
> *As I hand these pins around,*
> *May angel love keep them safe and sound.*
> *So mote it be.*

◆ Now give an angel brooch to each of your loved ones for protection and to help them make contact with their own guardian angels.

Make sure you wear your own brooch regularly.

Spell for angelic protection when driving

Purpose of ritual: To protect you as you drive.

Items required: None.

Lunar phase: Any.

Driving on Britain's roads can be a hazardous business. As soon as I passed my driving test a few years ago, I noticed for the first time what a hostile place the roads can be. As a learner, you are protected from this hostility and other drivers tend to give you more time and space, but once the L-plates come off, it can sometimes feel as if you are going into battle when all you want to do is drive safely across town. I decided that I would address this problem by calling on some magickal assistance and I came up with this simple incantation.

◆ Every time you get behind the wheel, repeat the following words, either out loud or in your head:

Guardian angels, protect and guide me. Let me drive well and safe, with harm to none, that I may return from my journey safe and sound. So mote it be.

Commit the incantation to memory and say it each time you are about to drive your car. I hope that it works as well for you as it has for me.

Spell to create an angelic bodyguard

Purpose of ritual: For personal protection when you are out and about.

Items required: None.

Lunar phase: Any.

Remember to take notice of any feelings of insecurity or vulnerability – don't just dismiss them.

◆ You can use this chant whenever you feel in particular need of protection or, alternatively, say it each time you leave home or work to go about your day.

> *Guardian angel, be with me,*
> *Wrap protective wings around me.*
> *Guide me away from possible harm,*
> *If danger is near, raise the alarm.*
> *Walk behind me and watch my back,*
> *Be the strength that I may lack.*
> *Guide me with your shining light,*
> *Defend me with your sword so bright.*
> *So mote it be.*

Once again, I recommend that you commit this chant to memory so you will have it on standby whenever you need it. This chant can either be said out loud or silently in your head if you prefer. This will not affect the power of the spell – the angels will hear you either way.

Following the feathers

So far in this book you have learnt how the angels can heal and uplift you, how they can assist you in your relationships and with finding love, and how they can help you to resolve any negative issues you may have. In this chapter you have also learnt how angels can protect you and deflect any negativity sent your way. In the next chapter we will be exploring how working with the angels can improve your prosperity and help you to achieve success. So, if you want to enjoy a bright and abundant future, read on.

A shimmering presence

A shimmering presence in the dark before dawn,
Heralds the birth of a babe, new born.
A feeling of peace and quiet serenity,
Gives hope to the hopeless, a future to see.
A calm found in chaos, a peace lingers on,
The disunited now working as one.
Harmony reigns where once was discord,
And love, like a waterfall, on humanity is poured.
The shimmering presence now changes shape and form
And a bright angel shelters the earth from the storm.

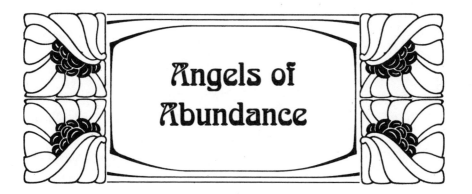

Angels of Abundance

Although angels are ethereal beings, they do understand the material world in which we live. They know that poverty is detrimental to our happiness, health and personal growth. If you let them, the angels can teach you the truth of universal abundance and they can help you to change your attitude towards your finances, your future and success in general.

The previous chapter looked at the concept of victim mentality and explored how your attitude can affect your life circumstances. Some people apply this victim mentality to their finances and overall prosperity, scrimping and saving, never fully enjoying the money that they do have, perhaps due to a deep internal belief that money is scarce and difficult to come by. They remain in an unfulfilling job, shelving their dreams and ambitions, believing that success is an unattainable goal. This kind of negative attitude is just the thing that prevents prosperity and abundance from being present in your life, so to improve your finances you must first of all improve your attitude towards abundance.

Money doesn't grow on trees

When you were young, how many times did your parents tell you that money doesn't grow on trees? At least once, I am sure. This gentle reprimand is a standard parenting tool used to teach us the value of money and to prevent us from becoming greedy or spoiled. The truth is, however, that money does grow on trees – paper money at least! A twenty-pound note is made from paper; paper is created from wood pulp and the wood is supplied by trees. Imagine for a moment that you had grown up being told this version of events and that money was widely available. How different would your attitude to money be today?

As an experiment, try telling yourself each day that money really does grow on trees and so it is freely available to all. Do this for at least a month and see how your attitude to money changes by the end of that time. Do you feel more abundant and in control of your financial destiny?

Most of us have been fed mixed messages regarding money, abundance and prosperity from the time that we were children. Our first experience of money usually comes via our parents and their financial attitude invariably helps to shape our own. As a result, we tend to carry these deep-seated attitudes and mixed messages through into adulthood. We may repeat old parental patterns, or cling to conditioned beliefs that hold us back rather than inspiring us to move forwards in our lives. On the other hand, we may be determined to do the opposite of everything our parents did in order to have a completely different lifestyle and financial destiny. Whatever their financial circumstances, most parents try to do their very best by their children, but when money is scarce, children often grow up with a poverty consciousness, believing abundance to be far out of their reach.

My childhood was a mixture of poverty and abundance. As the daughter of a redundant steel worker, I learnt at quite a young age the value of money, in that we never seemed to have enough of it! I can remember my parents worrying about how they would pay the bills. There were no savings in the bank, no exotic holidays abroad and we lived in a tiny terraced house that didn't even have a garden.

At the same time, though, we did experience feelings of abundance, for we had a car and we also had a caravan on the coast which meant that I spent a large part of my childhood by the sea. My friends all lived in big houses with large gardens, but I was the only one lucky enough to spend every weekend and holiday at the seaside.

I can remember the wonderful feelings of freedom and escape I experienced as I breathed in that first scent of sea air on arriving at the caravan. I didn't realise it at the time, but the days I spent there were my introduction to abundance, and one of my goals is still to live by the sea. I try to visit the coast as often as I can. Walking on the beach and listening to the waves immediately makes me feel uplifted, free and incredibly abundant.

Take a look back on your own childhood and adolescence and try to determine what messages and financial attitudes you were absorbing about prosperity. Did you feel abundant as a child, or were your parents struggling with poverty? It may be that you experienced both abundance and poverty, as I did. Spend some time thinking about your youth, your home and your family; think of how your parents related to money and how this may translate into your own current attitudes and lifestyle.

Triggering abundance

What is abundance? Is it money in the bank, holidays abroad, owning a house and holiday home, indulging in expensive hobbies, eating out at great restaurants, drinking champagne and fine wine? The truth is that abundance is none of these things, and at the same time, it can be all of them. This is because abundance is a very personal issue and so what makes one person feel abundant, may leave the next person feeling quite poverty stricken. At its core, abundance is a feeling, an emotion. While a nice car and a country cottage are lovely to have, they are only the external trappings of abundance, for true abundance exists in the spirit. This effectively means that it isn't what you have that makes you abundant, it's how you feel about what you have. Taking this on board means that you can feel abundant on any day of the week, regardless of your personal circumstances. You simply need to discover what it is that triggers this feeling of abundance for you personally.

Those of you who love retail therapy will have a clear understanding of temporary abundance, for this is the thrill you feel when you are out shopping. The problem is that if you are spending on credits cards then your experience of abundance is entirely false and you may well be digging yourself deep into debt. Also, once the initial shopping buzz has worn off, your mind may have a tendency to wander back to the shop and pine for all the things you didn't buy, leaving you feeling unsatisfied. Thus the cycle begins again and your quest for abundance could seem to be never ending.

The trick is to find ways to gain that abundant, prosperous feeling without racking up debt or spending a fortune. This depends upon discovering your personal abundance triggers, which are often quite simple things. So, before you move through the spells of this chapter, I want you to do some soul searching. Take a pen and note pad, and brainstorm, writing down all the things that make you feel abundant. This needn't be a list of material assets. Instead, try to include some things that you can enjoy quite cheaply and yet which still make you feel uplifted, prosperous and abundant. Here is my own list of abundance triggers by way of example:

- Being by the sea and walking on the beach. Sitting to watch the waves roll in and listen to the cry of the seagulls.
- Riding my horses, especially riding through woodlands and cross-country.
- Walking in the local woods or in the countryside.
- Walking in the wind and rain.
- Enjoying snowy days.
- Driving my car.
- Paying household expenses and bills.
- Grocery shopping and stocking up kitchen cupboards.
- Having a romantic meal cooked for me.
- Eating al fresco in the garden.
- A trip to the cinema, theatre or ballet.
- Relaxing in a bubble bath, sipping white wine. Using luxury bath products and toiletries.

◆ Indulging in a box of chocolates and a good DVD or novel.
◆ Filling the room with burning scented candles.
◆ Picking blackberries.
◆ Working in the garden.
◆ Taking time out to meditate and practise spell craft.
◆ Dancing and singing.
◆ Lazing on my four-poster bed and flipping through fashion magazines.
◆ Holidays in the Scottish Highlands.
◆ Working from home as a writer.

As you can see from this list, my feelings of abundance and prosperity do not rely on having unlimited funds. There are things that I can do to feel abundant that don't cost anything. A walk in the woods is free, so is picking the blackberries that grow at the bottom of my garden. Grocery shopping and paying bills are things that we must all do, so it costs no more to enjoy the abundance trigger within a kitchen full of goodies.

Make your own list and see what you come up with. Once you find your abundance triggers, it will be easier for you to feel abundant on a daily basis – simply by indulging in one of your trigger activities.

Ethics of prosperity magick

It is perfectly permissible to work magick to help yourself through a financial crisis or tight spot, providing you abide by the rules of prosperity magick. You already know that all positive magick is cast with harm to none, but this is especially important when it comes to prosperity magick. This is because money and prosperity can come to you in negative ways, for example, in the form of an inheritance following the death of a loved one or as compensation after an accident of some kind. So do make sure that your magick is cast in accordance with the Wiccan rede.

All the prosperity spells in this chapter use the angels as a focus so they are very gentle and positive in nature. But that is no excuse for you to be a lazy witch. Get into good habits now and they will stand you in good stead when you begin to create your own spells and rituals.

You should spellcast for only a little more than you actually need for comfort's sake, as this will bring about the best results. If you wish to be prosperous and you are in debt then it is vital that you address this issue. Work prosperity magick from new moon to full moon, and then work spells to tackle and banish your debt from full moon to dark moon. You will find both kinds of rituals in this chapter. You should, of course, take practical steps, such as cutting up credit cards and throwing away catalogues, as a way of backing up your magick and to break bad spending habits. Indulge in your less expensive abundance triggers instead.

When working prosperity magick regularly you will begin to feel more in control of your financial future. Try to work an abundance spell each full moon in order to keep the abundance flowing.

The money that you spell for will usually manifest in a very ordinary and routine way and you might not at first recognise that your spell has worked, so do be on the lookout for mundane abundance – an unexpected tax refund, a pay rise, overtime at work and so on. Once your finances start to turn around, keep up the good work in order to keep your financial life moving forwards in a positive direction.

Archangel Barakiel

Barakiel is one of the lesser know archangels. He is the angel of success, good fortune and abundance. Barakiel can turn your personal wheel of fortune in a positive direction and he can guide you on your personal path towards prosperity, abundance and success. He is the angel of the rising star, aiding and abetting those who wish to make it big in the limelight. Barakiel is the original talent scout, the celestial being who guides those who seek fame, fortune and celebrity, providing that they have some talent to recommend them, that is.

Barakiel's colours are green, gold, silver and white. He is associated with the stars, especially shooting stars, and attuning with his energies can encourage those of you who wish to become stars in your own right. Whoever you are, wherever you live, Barakiel wants you to shine in all that you do.

In addition, Barakiel can cut away the poverty trap, handing over a universal cheque of abundance instead. Visualise him walking along the Milky Way, bearing a pot of gold in the crook of one arm and scattering shooting stars from an out-stretched hand. He is swathed in robes of abundance – green, gold and silver – and his eyes are the colour of emeralds.

Ḫealing your financial mindset

In order to heal your financial life and enjoy the universal gifts of prosperity and abundance, you need to align your way of thinking to an attitude that welcomes abundance into your life. Initially, this means that you should express gratitude for all those things that you already have.

I realise that some of you will be living in situations that are far from your personal ideal, but in being grateful for what you do have, you will develop a positive attitude and so prosperity will begin to flow in your direction. As an example, have you ever bought someone a gift only to be faced with ingratitude? Did you feel that you had wasted your time, money and generosity on that person? This is exactly how the universal law works – it gives more freely to those who express gratitude and appreciation. So, be grateful for what you have and more will come to you.

Remember also that the world is a naturally abundant place. Poverty is man-made and caused largely by human greed. Make a conscious decision today to choose abundance instead.

Here is a simple chant to help you get things moving:

Barakiel, heal my mind,
Help me welcome gifts in kind.
Guide me forth and let me see
The world is full of prosperity.
I banish debt and vanquish strife,
I welcome abundance in my life.
For the free will of all and with harm to none,
In angel love, this spell is done.

Repeat this chant daily, especially when you feel yourself dwelling on thoughts of poverty or lack, or worrying about money in general.

Pathway to the pot of gold

The following meditation is based upon a special dream I had in which I found the pot of gold. I have used the meditation several times and it always leaves me feeling much more positive about my finances.

Find a quiet place to work, and sit comfortably. Tape the meditation in your own voice, if possible, or have a friend read it to you slowly. Breathe in a slow, controlled manner, until you feel calm and centred. Close your eyes and, in your mind, begin to visualise the following pathworking.

◆ You are standing in a poppy-filled meadow. The sky above is blue, and fluffy white clouds float by on the breeze. At the opposite side of the meadow is a country lane, and Barakiel is waiting for you there.

◆ You cross the meadow and make your way towards this magnificent angel. He is wearing a robe of deep forest-green, covered by a mantle made of gold cloth. As you get closer, you notice that his wings are formed from sparkling silver feathers and they glitter in the sunlight. Barakiel smiles at you, his green eyes shining in welcome. He takes your hand and leads you forward into the country lane.

◆ The first thing you notice is a change in the weather. The temperature drops and snowflakes begin to fall, although the sun is still shining and the trees are in full leaf and blossom. It is as if you are experiencing all four seasons at the same time. A breeze whips through your hair as you follow Barakiel down the country lane.

◆ On your right is a dry stone wall with the poppy meadow beyond; on your left is a steep drop down to a green valley below. The left side of the lane is lined with thick brambles and undergrowth that create a boundary between you and the valley. The snow is falling steadily, settling on the ground, yet all the plants are covered with blossom, berries and leaves. This confusion of the seasons creates the prettiest landscape you have ever seen. Smiling over the valley is a bright rainbow of shimmering colours. It is so close you could almost reach out and touch it.

◆ Walking on down the lane you pass by an ancient oak tree on the right side of the path. A little further on you pass a hawthorn tree white with blossom and snow. One of the hawthorn twigs has fallen and lies directly across your path. Barakiel turns and asks, 'Are you ready to accept prosperity into your life?' You nod your head and, smiling, Barakiel replies, 'Then step over the barrier and into abundance.' You step over the twig, taking care not to tread on the delicate white blossom.

◆ A little further down the lane you can see an ash tree and, with a gasp, you realise that you are standing by the three sacred trees of the faerie triad: oak, ash and thorn. All three trees are lined up on the right-hand side of the path. Barakiel walks down the lane until he is between the hawthorn and ash trees. He points to the undergrowth on the left-hand side of the lane and for the first time you notice a large iron cauldron tucked away in the brambles. The cauldron is filled with snow and, walking over, you dip in your hand and lift out a handful of soft snow. As you do so, the rainbow suddenly shimmers even brighter and the coloured arc seems to expand, ending right by the side of the cauldron. Looking down into your hand and the cauldron, you see that the snow has turned to gold dust – you realise that you have found the pot of gold at the end of the rainbow.

◆ 'You may make a single wish. Only one, so wish wisely,' says Barakiel. You close your eyes and make your wish, and on a puff of wind the gold dust in your hand is swept forth into the universe to manifest your wish.

◆ You stand up and turn to Barakiel who says, 'Know that this is a sacred space, a world between worlds. Four seasons exist as one, each equal in abundance. Those who recognise the faerie triad and see the beauty in winter's snow activate the rainbow and so discover the pot of gold.
The magick of this place will remain with you in your daily life. Look for the abundance in all things and know that you can return to me here whenever you wish.'

◆ Thank Barakiel and allow him to lead you back up the country lane and out into the meadow. Walk back into the middle of the poppy field, then turn and wave farewell to Barakiel who stands on the path waiting for your next visit. Become aware of your current surroundings and the present moment in time. Then, when you are ready, open your eyes.

Make a note of your meditational journey in your Book of Enlightenment, noting down what you wished for and taking care to date the entry. When your wish comes true be sure to make a note of how and when manifestation occurred.

Barakiel's prosperity box spell

Purpose of ritual: To bring prosperity and abundance into your life.

Items required: Patchouli incense stick, decorative angel trinket box, shiny 1p piece.

Lunar phase: New to full moon.

For this ritual you will need to find a decorative angel trinket box that really appeals to you. It needn't be an expensive item – you could even make a special box yourself and decorate it accordingly.

◆ Take the items required to your altar, and prepare as usual (see pages 60–1).

◆ Light the illuminator candles and the incense stick. Patchouli is magickally linked with prosperity and abundance, so smudge the trinket box by passing the incense stick all around the box, engulfing it in the fragrant smoke. Do this for a couple of minutes then allow the incense to burn down in an appropriate holder.

◆ Put the 1p coin in the box and say:

To Barakiel, this coin I send,
That abundance to me he will lend.
As I add a coin, day by day,
I ensure prosperity will come my way.

◆ Each day add a small denomination coin to the box and repeat the incantation. When the box is full, either deposit the money in your savings account or give it to a charity of your choice. Then begin to fill the box again. This will ensure that you are working towards abundance and prosperity on a daily basis. Be patient and have faith that the angel magick will work.

Emergency funds spell

Purpose of ritual: To spell for money in an emergency.

Items required: Slip of paper, silver pen, something that represents your need (such as an unpaid bill or a reminder letter), gold or silver angel statue, tea-light and holder.

Lunar phase: Any.

There may be times in your life when you need money quickly to cover an unexpected expense, or to pay a bill that is more than you budgeted for. In such a situation, an emergency money spell could be the answer.

◆ Take the items required to your angel altar, and prepare as usual (see pages 60–1).

◆ Settle at your altar and call on the aid of Barakiel in the following way:

> *Barakiel, I call you.*
> *I need your help today.*
> *Angel of prosperity,*
> *Please bring funds my way!*

◆ Using the silver pen, on the slip of paper, write down the amount of money you need for your emergency, what the money is for and the final date by which you need the funds.

◆ Sign the slip of paper and place it with the bill, or whatever, beneath the gold or silver angel statue.

◆ Place the tea-light in its holder directly in front of the angel, light the tea-light and say the following chant:

> *I have a need, it's written here.*
> *I've spelled my wish loud and clear.*
> *And now in trust I wait and see*
> *For I know this money comes to me.*
> *For the free will of all and with harm to none,*
> *By angel love, this spell is done.*

◆ Allow the tea-light to burn down.

You should soon have the means to pay your emergency expense.

Financial blessings spell

Purpose of ritual: To bless all your financial items.

Items required: Your purse or wallet, cheque book, recent bank statements, savings books and so on, lots of small angel stickers.

Lunar phase: Full moon.

This really simple spell will help to bring the blessings of the angels to all your financial transactions.

◆ Prepare for ritual as usual (see pages 60–1).

◆ Empower the angel stickers by holding your hands over them, palms down, and saying:

Guardian angel, Barakiel, angels of abundance, bestow your blessings and fortune through these stickers. Guide and protect all my financial transactions that I may continue to enjoy the unlimited abundance of the universe. So mote it be.

◆ Now apply the stickers to all your financial tools and paper work, placing them on the back of cheque books and bank statements, on the inside of your purse and so on. Make sure that every account and every aspect of your financial life is blessed with an angel sticker.

Your finances should begin to run more smoothly and any hiccups should be quickly sorted out.

Spell to keep money in your purse

Purpose of ritual: To ensure that money stays in your purse.

Items required: Scissors, silver construction paper or thin card, gold pen, patchouli oil, your purse or wallet.

Lunar phase: Full moon.

◆ Prepare for ritual in the usual way (see pages 60–1).

◆ Spend a few moments at your angel altar concentrating on Barakiel and his gifts of prosperity and abundance. Know that you will never really be left wanting.

◆ Carefully cut out a feather shape from the silver card.

◆ Using the gold pen, write the name Barakiel on one side, and on the other side:

My purse is never empty,
All my needs are always met.

◆ Anoint the silver feather with a dab of patchouli oil at each end and then place the feather in your purse to attract prosperity.

Spell to see abundance in all things

Purpose of ritual: To help you to accept universal abundance.

Items required: None.

Lunar phase: Any.

The following incantation is designed to help you see the natural abundance and prosperity of the universe. It will help to heal your negative perceptions of money.

◆ For the best results, say the following chant each morning as you dress and prepare for the day ahead:

The sun is shining golden,
The stars are bright as silver,
The earth grows green in leaf and life,
And for all our needs, the earth provides.
The clouds spill out their nurturing rain,
The boughs yield forth their fruit,
The angels guide my daily dance,
And fill my life with sweet abundance.
Blessed be.

Banishing debt

In order to heal your financial life you may have to deal with the issue of debt. While racking up a huge credit card bill and then burying your head in the sand might work for a short while, you will have to face up to it eventually.

Remember that 'to heal' means 'to bring about a state of balance'. All the money spells in the world won't help if you continue to spend what you don't have. So begin to tip the scales in your favour by putting credit cards beyond the reach of temptation, throwing away catalogues, avoiding junk mail and so on. Then set up a savings account and begin to save however much you can afford each month. Even a small sum will soon add up to a reasonable amount and this will act as a financial cushion. Just knowing that you have some savings can greatly enhance your sense of financial security. Now deal with your existing debts by making regular payments and using the following spells to give yourself a magickal edge.

Spell to freeze your debts

Purpose of ritual: To prevent your debts from escalating.

Items required: Evidence of your debts (bills, letters and so on), slip of card, black pen, plastic tub and lid, small angel charm, three white feathers.

Lunar phase: Waning moon.

◆ Take all the items required to your angelic altar, and prepare for ritual in the usual way (see pages 60–1).

◆ Sit for a while and contemplate the issue. Know that you can never be truly prosperous when you are up to your eyes in high-interest debt. Accept responsibility and make the decision to get out of debt as soon as you can.

◆ Place all your debt papers in a pile and add up the total amount owed. Using the black pen, write this sum on the slip of card, followed by the words:

Barakiel, please freeze this debt and help me to make prompt
and regular payments. I ask for your assistance to heal this
aspect of my financial life. So mote it be.

◆ Place the slip of card in the tub and add the angel charm and the three white feathers.

◆ Fill the tub with water to cleanse any negativity attached to the debt, put on the lid and place the tub at the back of the freezer to freeze the debt.

◆ Do not allow the tub to defrost until you have paid off the debts. Once you are debt-free, take out the tub, let the water melt and bury the spell items in the garden.

◆ Do not run up new debts but enjoy your new-found prosperity.

Spell to be free of the poverty trap

Purpose of ritual: To escape from poverty.

Items required: White candle and holder, inscribing tool, silver altar bell.

Lunar phase: Full moon.

There are many things that can contribute towards the poverty trap: credit cards and debt, unemployment, illness, living on benefits and so on. While the situation is not necessarily your fault, if you remain complacent about it you will never break free. So be proactive – find out what education and career opportunities excite and inspire you, start a small home-based business, go self-employed, pay off debts, find a better job. Start to think of yourself as an entrepreneur! Then work this spell to give yourself a magickal kick-start out of the poverty trap.

◆ Prepare for ritual in the usual way (see pages 60–1).

◆ Take the white candle and, beginning at the wick, inscribe the words 'poverty trap', followed by your name, down the length of the candle.

◆ On the other side of the candle, inscribe 'Barakiel, set me free'.

◆ Set the candle in its holder and light it.

◆ As it burns, chant:

In the poverty trap I will not be,
For Barakiel sets me free!

◆ Each time you repeat the chant, ring the altar bell once to ring in the changes in your life. Continue with this for as long as you remain focused. Then allow the candle to burn down naturally.

◆ Clear away and go about your day.

'Flush it!' spell

Purpose of ritual: To flush away a debt or financial problem.

Items required: Toilet paper, black marker pen.

Lunar phase: Any.

This quick spell will soon help you get to grips with financial hiccups.

◆ Write the nature of the debt or problem on a sheet of toilet paper using the black marker pen and then flush it down the toilet to be rid of it. Simple!

◆ Repeat daily until the problem has been resolved.

Moving into abundance

Once you have healed your financial life, remember to keep your thoughts of abundance positive. Money is just energy and, as such, it can never be taken away or lost; it simply changes form and shape. Work consistently to pull this energy towards you by accepting the natural abundance of the world and by dealing with personal debt. Then think prosperously and welcome universal abundance into your life.

Bridge of angels

Take me over the bridge of angels
To my loved ones dear.
Let them know, although I've gone,
My spirit lingers near.
Take me over the bridge of angels
That I may hear them laugh,
Share their triumphs and their joy
And guide them on their path.
Take me over the bridge of angels
That I may calm their fears,
Pick them up when they fall
And wipe away their tears.
Take me to the bridge of angels
To meet loved ones of mine,
That I may ease their crossing
And tell them it's their time.
Dancing on the bridge of angels,
Together again, you and me!
Spirit to spirit, heart to heart,
We dance into eternity!

Angels of Magick

Angels adore magickal practitioners. This is largely because those who practise magick and witchcraft tend to be proactive individuals who take personal responsibility for realising their own dreams and ambitions. As practising witches, we do not wait around for the good things in life to be handed to us on a silver platter; we take charge of our lives and control our own destiny as much as humanly possible. This means that we work healing magick to bring balance to all aspects of our lives and to iron out any wrinkles that may be causing us problems. Having said that, even witches can benefit from a little extra help every now and then, and this is where the angels, particularly Uriel, come in.

Archangel Uriel

Archangel Uriel is the divine magician and enchanter of the angelic dimensions. He is the great sorcerer of the celestial realms and he is thought to be the guardian angel and protector of witches and magickal practitioners. Uriel is linked with knowledge and is therefore sometimes depicted reading a scroll or a book. He presides over all aspects of magickal practice as well as dreams, divination, prophecy and magickal writings. He is the angel of the mysteries, helping the universe to keep its secrets, while at the same time he guides humankind on its gradual quest for knowledge, ensuring that we are in a position to receive the considerable wisdom he bestows.

In some traditions, Uriel is known as Ariel, and although these are actually two different celestial beings, they do share similar traits, and in recent times the two are often considered to be almost interchangeable. In my personal practice of angel craft, I see Uriel as being masculine in energy and Ariel as being more feminine. Ariel is closely linked to the earth elementals and nature spirits, so if faerie magick appeals to you, try communing with Ariel.

Both Uriel and Ariel are closely linked with Mother Nature and the earth and they are sometimes referred to as 'earth angels', being the celestial guardians of our planet. In view of this, they are definitely the angels to invoke when performing any kind of conservation or planetary awareness magick. They are also great guardians for endangered species or places of natural beauty – so invoke Uriel and Ariel to keep the bulldozer at bay.

Uriel is the angel of winter. His direction is north, his magickal hour is the witching hour of midnight and his most sacred time is the midwinter festival, the winter solstice. Uriel is linked with the element of earth so if you were born into the astrological signs of Taurus, Virgo or Capricorn, then Uriel is already watching over you and guiding you on your path, so you could already enjoy a natural affinity with this angel.

In my own practice of angel craft, I associate Archangel Uriel with the bridge of angels: the ethereal bridge between ourselves and our deceased loved ones. In this role, Uriel can help people to connect with loved ones who have crossed over, carrying messages of comfort, love and wisdom back and forth across the bridge. In this task, he is assisted by the Gothic angels and personal guardian angels. In addition, Uriel can help people to experience visitation dreams and can nurture the love which transcends the spirit bridge, through the veil of death.

With his strong links to magick and death, it should come as no great surprise to learn that Uriel is considered to be the angel of the otherworld or underworld. He can guide your astral travels, send

special messages to you via your dreams and help yo
with your spirit guide and power animals (real
creatures with which you feel a strong affinity).

Visualise Uriel coming into your circle on the north wind,
wearing billowing robes of purple, magenta, plum, silver and smoky
grey. His wings are as white as winter's snow and a full midnight
moon rides high in the starry sky behind him. His feet are wreathed
in holly and ivy, symbolising his link with the winter months and
the winter solstice sabbat. In his hands, he unrolls the scroll of
wisdom from which he teaches the magickal mysteries to all those
who are willing to learn.

Angels of the zodiac

Whatever your zodiac sign, there are associated angels who perfectly
understand your strengths, traits and weaknesses. Below is a basic
run down of all the zodiac angels. If you are put off by the orthodox
names of these celestial beings, then simply call on 'the angels of
Scorpio' and so on. It is, after all, an energy you are invoking, not a
specific name.

♈ Aries

The angels Michael, Aiel and Sariel are associated
with this sign. They will nurture your courage and
leadership qualities while keeping any bullying
tendencies under control.

♉ Taurus

The angels Uriel, Ariel and Asmodel govern the sign
of Taurus. They can help you to nurture your patience,
reliability and emotional stability. Taureans can have a
tendency to be bull-headed so call on your zodiac
angels to assist you in overcoming this problem.

♊ Gemini

The angels of Gemini are Raphael, Ambriel and Saraiel. They will help you to demonstrate your playful, fun-loving nature and can prevent you from becoming reckless or foolhardy.

♋ Cancer

The angels Gabriel, Cael and Muriel are linked with this sign. Call on their protection when you feel vulnerable or to enhance your natural caution and hone your instincts. They can also help you to venture out into the world and to strengthen your worldly shell.

♌ Leo

The angels of Leo are Michael, Verchiel and Seratiel. Call on them to enhance your strength and loyalty, and to prevent you from becoming self-centred.

♍ Virgo

The angels Uriel, Hamaliel and Schaltiel are the governing angels of Virgo. They can help you in your daily tasks, encouraging a hard-working, conscientious attitude. At the same time, they can prevent your perfectionist tendencies from taking over.

♎ Libra

The angels of Libra are Raphael, Zuriel and Hadakiel. Call on them to enhance your sense of justice and balance, and to prevent indecision.

♏ Scorpio

Gabriel, Bariel and Barchiel are associated with Scorpio. Invoke their energies to enhance your self-empowerment and independent spirit. Call on their assistance to help you deal with suspicion and jealousy.

♐ Sagittarius

The angels Michael, Advachiel and Saritaiel are linked with the sign of Sagittarius. They can help you to nurture your optimism, compassionate nature and love of animals. They can also prevent you from becoming judgmental and over-confident.

♑ Capricorn

Uriel, Haniel and Semakiel are all linked with the sign of Capricorn. Call on their assistance to achieve your ambitions and to strive for success. At the same time, they can help to keep you grounded in reality and will keep any 'pie in the sky' ideas under control.

♒ Aquarius

Raphael, Cambiel and Ausiel are linked with this sign and can help you to enhance your determination and drive, offering guidance and direction. Call on them to keep stubbornness under control.

♓ Pisces

The angels Gabriel, Pasiel and Barakiel govern the sign of the fish. They will help you to go with the flow of life and to empathise with others. Call on their aid to prevent a tendency towards melancholy.

Spell to invoke assistance from your zodiac angels

Purpose of ritual: To bring help from your angels.

Items required: White card, silver pen, scissors, large envelope.

Lunar phase: Full moon.

- Prepare for ritual in the usual way (see pages 60–1).
- Settle down at your angelic altar and breathe deeply until you feel centred.
- Think of the issue that you require angelic assistance with and visualise the positive outcome of the situation.
- Draw a large angel shape on the white card and cut it out.
- On the front of the card write the name of your chosen zodiac angel, and then decorate the angel with the appropriate zodiac symbol. On the back of the card write the nature of the issue you need help with. You can use more than one angel if you wish.
- Hold the angel in your hands and continue to visualise a positive outcome.
- Chant the following incantation seven times:

  Zodiac angels of the stars, guardians of this sign,
  I call on your assistance with this problem of mine.

- Once you have finished chanting, place the angel in the envelope and seal it. Leave the envelope on your altar until the issue has been resolved, then burn it and give thanks to the zodiac angels.

Angel dreams ritual

Purpose of ritual: To petition Uriel for answers or solutions.

Items required: Sheet of notepaper or an angel note card, pen.

Lunar phase: Any.

Archangel Uriel is strongly associated with dreams, visions, the imagination, all aspects of the subconscious mind and the higher self. Sometimes Uriel will send us messages via our dreams, giving guidance as we sleep, helping us to deal with our personal issues and even allowing us a glimpse of all that we might become if we follow our true path in life. This nocturnal connection can work both ways, meaning that you can petition Uriel to provide an answer to your question or solution to a problem, via your dreams.

◆ Write a brief letter to Uriel, outlining your current problem or the situation you need help with.

◆ Sign the letter and then below write:

> *Uriel, high in the realm of Unseen,*
> *Give me guidance within my dreams.*
> *In nocturnal visions I wish to see,*
> *The best way forward, so mote it be.*

◆ Say this incantation before you go to sleep at night and put the letter inside your pillowcase, beneath the pillow.

You should receive angelic insight in your dreams within the next seven nights.

Angel crystal divination spell

Purpose of ritual: To create and use a divination tool.

Items required: Small pouch, lavender essential oil, angel brooch, one each of the following crystals: amethyst, aventurine, carnelian, citrine, iron pyrites (fool's gold), clear quartz, rose quartz, smoky quartz.

Lunar phase: Full moon.

◆ Prepare for ritual in the usual way (see pages 60–1) and place all the items required on the pentacle on your altar.

◆ Concentrate on the energies of Archangel Uriel. Ask that he assist you in your magick tonight and always.

◆ Now hold your hands over the crystals and say:
In the name of Archangel Uriel, I bless these crystals, that they may become a tool of divination and insight. So mote it be.

◆ Pin the angel brooch to the pouch and put the crystals inside one by one, then sprinkle the whole thing with a few drops of lavender oil.

◆ Leave the pouch in place for a full moon cycle. On the next full moon, your new divination tool will be fully charged and ready to use.

◆ Once the pouch has been charged, hold it in your hands and concentrate on your question or the issues that you require insight into.

◆ When you are ready, draw out one of the crystals and discover your answer, using the interpretations below:

Amethyst

Archangel Uriel is urging you to feel the power of magick that you hold within you and to allow enchantment into your life.

Aventurine

A healing process is taking place in your life right now. It may be that you need to work harder towards a state of balance and equilibrium. Archangel Raphael is guiding you through this.

Carnelian

Fiery carnelian represents Archangel Michael; you are being guided and defended on your path. Be assured that you are never without protection.

Citrine

Archangel Jophiel is urging you to get in touch with your creative side. Feel the inspiration and release the artist, dancer, musician or writer in you. Be creative in your thinking and your general attitude to life.

Iron pyrites

This crystal represents Barakiel and his lessons of abundance. Remember that true abundance does not come from money, but only by accepting the unlimited abundance of nature. You may experience a financial windfall – spend it wisely.

Clear quartz

This crystal represents your guardian angel who is always looking out for you. Remember that he cannot help unless you ask; you are being reminded to ask for assistance when you need it and to keep the faith.

Rose quartz

Make space and time in your life for love and romance. Enjoy your loved ones. If you are single, then find new ways to explore and indulge your romantic side. Archangel Gabriel is reminding you to feel and share the love.

Smoky quartz

Darkness, depression and uncertainty may surround you, but the Gothic angels can lead you out into the light if you let them.

Spell to find a magickal mentor

Purpose of ritual: To meet someone of a like mind with whom you can enjoy magick.

Items required: Purple candle and holder, inscribing tool.

Lunar phase: New moon.

A magickal life can be lonely if you have no one with whom you can share your new passion. Old friends may have no interest in magick and potential new friends and romantic interests may be put off by this aspect of your life. I do not recommend declaring yourself a witch until you have got to know people quite well.

While being a solitary practitioner offers you incredible freedom, it is always nice to have someone with whom you can share ideas, sabbats, the ritual wine and a gossip about all things crafty. This spell will open the door for such individuals to come into your life, but you need to back it up by getting out there and meeting people. Strike up a conversation at your local New Age shop, go to Wiccan festivals and attend moots. You never know who the angel of destiny has waiting for you.

◆ Prepare for ritual in the usual way (see pages 60–1).
◆ Take the purple candle and inscribe your name on one side. On the other side inscribe the words 'Magickal friend and mentor'.
◆ Place the candle in the holder and light the wick.
◆ Now sit comfortably, focusing on the flame and begin to chant the following:

> *People who are like in mind,*
> *Of gracious heart and spirit kind,*
> *Come to me before the moon does wane.*
> *I cast this spell in Uriel's name.*

You should begin to meet more like-minded people within the lunar cycle. Your ideal friend or mentor may not come immediately, but it won't be long before he or she is drawn towards you. Be patient, be safe when meeting strangers, and have fun.

Spell to incubate a visitation dream

Purpose of ritual: To experience a visitation dream from a deceased loved one.

Items required: Stick of your favourite incense, the deceased's favourite fragrance (if she or he had one), photo of the deceased, your Book of Enlightenment, pen, tea-light with a holder.

Lunar phase: Any.

Angels are thought to be able to cross the boundaries between the living and the dead and they can be a comfort to the bereaved. Sometimes we may feel the need to reconnect with our loved ones who have passed over, and our dreams are the ideal place to do this.

In our dreams, reality is suspended for a while, and that which could never be in the real world can easily take place in our dreams – if you have ever dreamed of a passionate embrace with Brad Pitt, you will know that this is true! Dream incubation is trying to bring about a very specific dream, and this spell is designed to incubate a dream of your loved one.

◆ Set up your bedroom so that it is as cosy and comforting as possible.

◆ Burn the incense and spray a little of the fragrance on your pillow. Place the photo of your loved one by the bed, along with your Book of Enlightenment and the pen. You will need these to record the details of your dream as soon as you wake up. This will make it easier to pick up any hidden symbols and messages in your dream.

◆ Have your ritual bath and then get ready for bed. In your bedroom, light the tea-light and say:

I call on Uriel to help me cross the bridge of angels.

◆ Spend some time thinking of your loved one and all that you would say to him or her. If tears come, just let them flow.

◆ Allow the candle to burn for a while and when you feel ready, begin to chant this incantation:

As I lay in slumber deep,
Take me forth within my sleep.
Between the times of now and then,
Let our spirits meet again.
Within the darkness of my dream,
My loved one comes on Uriel's beam.

◆ Repeat the incantation seven times then blow out the candle and get into bed.

◆ Keep chanting softly as you fall asleep. Do not worry if you do not experience a visitation that same night; it can sometimes take a while for the message to get through, though the spell should work within seven nights. Remember to write down the details of the dream as soon as you wake up.

Once you have opened the psychic gates of your dreams you might find that your loved ones tend to pop in unannounced on occasion. This is one of the greatest gifts of living a magickal life, so take comfort in these visitation dreams and know that your loved ones are still watching over you.

Uriel's boon spell

Purpose of ritual: To ask for a favour from Archangel Uriel.

Items required: Pen, notepad, envelope, cauldron or heatproof dish.

Lunar phase: New moon.

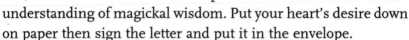

◆ Prepare for ritual in the usual way (see page 60–1).

◆ Once you are settled at your altar, begin to put your request into words by writing a letter to Uriel asking for your chosen boon. This can be anything you like, from career success to a deeper understanding of magickal wisdom. Put your heart's desire down on paper then sign the letter and put it in the envelope.

◆ Hold the letter over your heart, close your eyes and say:

> *Uriel of wisdom deep,*
> *The key to my dreams I know you keep.*
> *I send these words through the fire,*
> *Please grant to me my heart's desire.*
> *So mote it be.*

◆ Light the envelope and allow it to burn in the cauldron.

◆ Scatter the ashes out of doors and wait for your boon to manifest.

Uriel's mirror-scrying spell

Purpose of ritual: To ask for Uriel's help when scrying.

Items required: Large mirror preferably of angelic design or dark glass scrying mirror, candle or tea-light, your Book of Enlightenment, pen.

Lunar phase: Any.

Scrying is the art of magickal seeing, when witches use their inner eyes to catch glimpses of the past, present and future. Most witches use a dark scrying mirror for this purpose, but you can also use an ordinary mirror, providing the room is darkened. Choose your mirror with care. One that hangs on the wall near a cosy chair will mean that you can sit comfortably while scrying. If your mirror has a decorative frame of angelic design, then so much the better.

◆ Dim the lights and light a single candle or tea-light, making sure that the flame is not directly reflected in the mirror.

◆ Sit quietly and call on Uriel's aid in the following way:

> *Uriel, fly on wings of light,*
> *Bring to me second sight.*
> *Between the worlds of here and there,*
> *Let the glass its secrets share.*
> *Scrying wisdom reveals to me*
> *That which I am meant to see.*

◆ Settle back and begin your scrying session, allowing your gaze to relax and making a mental note of any pictures, words or images that come into your mind. Don't worry if you don't see anything in the mirror itself; often scrying visions come to us in our mind and these images are just as valid.

◆ The first hint of a physical vision is when the scrying vehicle, in this case the mirror, becomes cloudy and seems to fill with smoke. Once the smoke clears, a physical vision should be seen within the mirror. This does take lots and lots of practice, but don't give up, just keep trying and make a note of all your scrying sessions in your Book of Enlightenment.

Earth angel spell

Purpose of ritual: To call on the power of the earth angels for a specific cause.

Items required: Pen and paper, angel trinket box.

Lunar phase: New to full moon.

If you need magickal help to heal a pet, to grow a beautiful garden, to protect an animal or a natural area, then call on Uriel and Ariel, the earth angels.

◆ Prepare as usual (see pages 60–1).

◆ Write down the issue you require help with on the slip of paper.

◆ Hold the paper and concentrate on a positive outcome for the situation. Repeat the following incantation seven times:

Uriel and Ariel,
Lend your powers to this spell.
Angels of the planet Earth,
Energise this magick's birth.
Assist with what is written here.
I call you now from far and near.
So mote it be.

◆ Place the spell paper in the trinket box and leave it in place on your altar until manifestation has occurred.

Following the feathers

As you can see from this chapter, working with Uriel will help you to bring magick into your life in a simple and accessible way. By working regularly with the angels of magick you will discover that your everyday life can become quite enchanting and you should soon be meeting people of a like mind, attuning with the angels of your birth sign and divining the future.

In the next chapter we will be looking at how the angels can inspire you to free your creativity, so if you have ever had dreams of writing a book, starting a rock band, becoming a dancer or hosting an exhibition of your artwork, then read on.

White feathers falling

White feathers falling,
The angels are calling,
Calling, calling out to you.
Silver bells ringing,
The angels are singing,
Singing, singing their song to you.
Wispy clouds streaming,
The angels are dreaming,
Dreaming, dreaming peace into you.
Soft moonlight gleaming,
The angels are beaming,
Beaming, beaming their smiles on you.
Bright sunlight around you,
The angels surround you,
All around angel love surrounding you.

Angels of Creativity and Inspiration

One of the most valuable gifts the angels give us is that of inspiration. Over the years, great works of art have been painted, beautiful poems have been written and films and TV shows have been produced, all on an angel theme. From Raphael and Botticelli to William Blake and John Milton, from *It's a Wonderful Life* and *City of Angels* to *Highway to Heaven* and the whitelighters in *Charmed*, the perception of angels has inspired them all.

The ancient Greeks believed that daimons were guardian angels who specifically inspired poets, philosophers, musicians and artists of every kind. Many creative people talk about their 'muse' descending upon them, meaning that they are feeling particularly inspired at that moment in time and that their project is going well. Even before the time of written language, humankind was inspired to create cave paintings and prehistoric artwork, so it would seem that we quite naturally feel the need to express ourselves creatively.

For some people, the creative juices are so rich that they feel compelled to make their living in a creative way. Professional authors, poets, journalists, artists, dancers, musicians, actors and craft workers all make their living by putting a monetary value on their inspiration and creative ideas and abilities. We may take pleasure in seeing a new film or exhibition, reading a new book or visiting the ballet; in this way, we are inspired and society as a whole is enriched by the talents of creative artists. For those who make their living working in the Arts, inspiration is a close, and sometimes fickle, friend.

For others, creative projects provide a pleasant weekend hobby, something to indulge in outside work or when the kids have gone to bed. In some cases, a creative talent is used to save money – think of all the knitting that goes on to clothe a new baby. It would seem that each and every one of us is blessed with some kind of talent or creative outlet. So, whether you enjoy cooking in the kitchen, singing in the bathroom or writing in your diary, some degree of inspiration is involved.

Personally, I do not believe that there is any such thing as a talentless individual – although you might not have the talent you most want. Not everyone has the skills to be able to make it as a pop star, a prima ballerina or a best-selling author. In discovering what your individual talent is, however, you will be able to free your creative energies in a positive and productive manner and Jophiel can help you do this.

Archangel Jophiel

The angel of inspiration and creativity is Archangel Jophiel. To me, her energies feel very feminine in nature. She is the voice of inspiration whispering in your ear and she can guide you on your creative path. She is the angel you should call on when a project you have been working on has stalled or if you are experiencing the dreaded writer's block. Jophiel also sends visions of all that you could be creatively through your dreams; so, if you dream that you have a record deal and are cutting your first album, this could be Jophiel urging you to go for it and follow your dreams. Jophiel wants people to understand that they were given their talents for a reason. If you have a great imagination or a lovely singing voice, her message is that you should do something with it. Make the very most of your talents as you never know where they will take you.

Being linked with creativity, Jophiel is usually depicted bearing either a musical instrument or a quill pen. She presides over the Arts and she can be attuned within any theatre, art gallery or other creative space. She encourages artists to join together and share their passion for their work, feeding off one another, whether this be in the manner of the famous Bloomsbury Group or via the more modern medium of e-mail and the internet. She is the voice that encourages you to sign up for a watercolour class or a dance class. She may inspire you to join a theatre group, to visit the ballet or even join the circus. She guides you to read the right books at the right time. She wants you to find joy in your own creativity and gain pleasure from the talents of others.

Jophiel's colours are soft pink and rich gold, so visualise her sweeping into your circle on fluffy white clouds, wearing floating robes of sunset pink and gold. Her wings have the golden tones of the sunset too, and she carries with her the tools of your chosen creative activity. At her feet are scattered books, artists' palettes and brushes, musical instruments and sheet music, theatrical masks and dance shoes. Words of inspiration and encouragement fall from her lips in soft dulcet tones, and she can work the miracle you may need to get your lucky break.

Inspirational writing

As I mentioned earlier, angels have been the inspiration behind hundreds of books, plays and poems. If the written word is where your own creativity lies then attuning with Jophiel can help you to create inspirational writing. Whether it's your dream to become a published writer or if your writing is very personal to you and you would much rather not share it with the world, it is putting pen to paper in order to express yourself that counts.

The angels of creativity can help you in your writing ventures, especially if you happen to be writing about the angels. When I wrote my book *Faerie Magick*, I found the project quite challenging, and although I have written several books over the past few years, I found that one to be the most difficult, namely because I was trying to pin down ethereal beings. As any faerie enthusiast will know, elementals are renowned for their trickiness, and it was a challenge to portray their otherworldly charm and enchantment in a down-to-earth way. Interestingly, the final chapter of *Faerie Magick*, which is about angels, was the easiest to write. Writing *Angel Craft and Healing* has been a smooth work in progress too and I can only imagine that the angels are more co-operative than the faeries were! I mention this to let you know that the words don't always come easily to me either and sometimes I have to chase them.

If you do have aspirations to become a writer, then attuning with angels of inspiration might help you on your way. You can also tap into Jophiel's energies in order to gain insight and guidance via the written word. This may take the form of written channelling (when you receive information from a higher source, see page 178) or a personal diary, or you may find that just the right type of reading material falls into your lap. Diary writing can be very therapeutic and is a great way to express yourself, getting all your negative thoughts and feelings down on paper and freeing up the space in your head for much nicer things. Writing poetry can be used in a similar way and because it is more abstract, you need not worry about hurting the feelings of anyone who you may have written about and who happens to read it.

The following rituals will help you on your way to using your imagination to its full potential.

Scroll of destiny ritual

Purpose of ritual: To call for angelic assistance with creative goals and ambitions.

Items required: Long sheet of paper (wallpaper is ideal), pen, one pink and one gold ribbon.

Lunar phase: New to full moon.

This ritual is for those of you who have creative ambitions, whether they are to be a singer, rock star, dancer or writer.

◆ Prepare for your spell craft in the usual way (see pages 60–1) and then settle down at your angel altar.

◆ Unroll the length of paper and, at the top, write:

Archangel Jophiel and angels of creativity, inspiration and ambition, please help me to manifest the following:

◆ Underneath, write a detailed account of what your ultimate creative ambition is. Keep your writing positive, so do not refer to any of the obstacles that may stand in your way, but write down your dream destiny in the present tense as if you are already living it. So, for example, write 'Last night I won the Booker Prize' rather than 'One day I would like to be nominated for the Booker Prize'. Keep your writing positive and be as detailed as you can about your destiny. Imagine that what you are writing about is happening to you right now – you are living your dream. If you can't even imagine living your dream, then how can you expect to create it as a reality?

◆ Once you have written out your destiny, sign and date it, then read it out loud to yourself and allow yourself to experience the excitement of living this reality.

◆ Roll the paper up and tie it with the pink and gold ribbons.

◆ Hold the scroll over your heart and chant the following incantation seven times:

I call Archangel Jophiel
Help me make this vision real.
Colour my dream with every hue,
Help me make my dreams come true.
My talent I want the world to see.
Please help me create my destiny!
So mote it be.

◆ Kiss the scroll and leave it on your altar.

◆ Read it out loud to yourself every night before you go to sleep, thus reaffirming your chosen destiny and increasing your chances of success.

Ritual to channel the written word

Purpose of ritual: To channel angelic messages.

Items required: Candle or tea-light and holder, stick of your favourite incense, CD of angel-inspired music (see page 201 for ideas), notebook, pen.

Lunar phase: Any.

Channelling is the art of receiving and passing on information from a higher source, in this case, the angelic dimensions. Some people claim to be able to channel through ghosts and spirit guides, as well as elemental beings. Those who do this on a regular basis are called mediums.

This ritual will enable you to solicit guidance from the angels by channelling the written word. As I mentioned earlier, the angels will love to help you with your writing, and channelling simply takes this one step further.

You may find that when writing with the angels, your work goes more smoothly, that the stream of words continues to flow through you without any blocks or long pauses. It may be that you cannot write or type fast enough and find it difficult to keep up with the words, that you use words outside of your normal vocabulary or write in a style that seems alien to you and yet at the same time is very comforting and almost familiar. However the words come, do not try to hold on to them or examine them, just let them flow onto the page.

You do not need to be at your altar for this ritual, so if you prefer to be out of doors in the garden then that's fine. Likewise, if you prefer to use a computer rather than a notepad, then that's okay too.

◆ Wherever you choose to work the ritual, set the scene by lighting the candle and incense and playing some angel-inspired music.

◆ Settle down and breathe deeply a few times until you feel calm and centred. Close your eyes and try to clear your mind.

◆ When you are ready, say:

> *Jophiel, angel of creativity,*
> *Inspire the words I write this day.*

◆ Only when you feel compelled to do so should you pick up the pen and start writing. Keep writing for as long as you can. Try not to think too much about what you are doing. Don't hold on to the words, or worry about spelling and grammar, just let the words flow through you and out onto the page or screen. Remember that the idea is to allow the angels to speak through you and, to do this, you need to relinquish control. Let your hand move across the page or the keyboard but don't try to direct it. When you feel that you have finished, stop.

◆ Read back over what you have written; it may be a letter, a poem or a piece of prose, or just a list of key words or ideas.

◆ Keep you written channelling notes somewhere safe; if it doesn't make any sense now, look at it again in six months' time and you may find that it will have more meaning.

Channelling is a skill that takes time to master. You are unlikely to gain the most valuable insights on your first try, so the more you practise, the more open the channel becomes, making it easier for angelic messages and information to come through. Try to channel through your angels at least once every couple of weeks. Over time, your skills will develop and you should begin to receive more detailed and accurate messages.

Feminine creativity

Women tend to be naturally creative, indulging in arts and crafts from quite a young age. Many women enjoy cooking and baking; some enjoy needlework or knitting. Still others find that their passion leans towards dance, performance art and so on.

Creativity is not necessarily about painting pictures or writing books. You are being creative when you bake cookies with the kids, or when you teach your grandchildren how to knit or make dolls clothes. Many women express themselves creatively through their wardrobe, bringing inspiration to the clothes they wear and developing a certain flair and style of their own.

Of course, we all know that a woman's greatest act of creativity comes when she has children. Giving birth to a baby is a sacred experience, yet motherhood can also mark the end of a woman's hobbies and pastimes, not to mention her independence. By the very nature of their helplessness and dependence, a baby or young child tends to take up all of its mother's valuable time and energy. But you owe it to yourself to maintain some aspect of the life you lived before.

This seems to be one area where the men do better than the women, as no matter how many changes a man goes through – engagement, marriage, fatherhood, even divorce – he still manages to turn up on the football field with his mates or for a round of golf with his dad. Take a leaf out of your man's book and insist on some time for yourself to indulge in your own creative pastimes. The solitude of motherhood may mean that you have little else to talk about, but nothing is more boring than a woman who can only talk about her children. Give yourself a break and find a hobby, and use the following spell to give you a boost.

Time out spell

Purpose of ritual: To encourage mothers to take time out.

Items required: Tea-light and holder.

Lunar phase: New to full moon.

This is a quick spell that will fit into your busy day.

◆ Light the tea-light, focus on the flame and repeat the following incantation:

> *Jophiel, inspire me and help me find the time*
> *To free my creativity and allow myself to shine.*
> *Help me to step out from the shadow of my kids*
> *And indulge in all the things I've begun to really miss.*
> *Send each and every mother a little time and space*
> *To be true unto herself and live her life with grace.*
> *So mote it be.*

◆ Allow the tea-light to burn down and schedule in some me-time.

Creative celebration

When people have something to celebrate, their creative juices naturally start to flow. Think of all the birthday cakes and wedding cakes that you have enjoyed over the years. The news of a family pregnancy sets off a veritable frenzy of knitting as friends and family members create bootees and bonnets galore, expressing their joy at the prospect of a new arrival.

Taking the time to create something out of nothing is still the most touching act of celebration, despite the consumerism of the world in which we live. If a new boyfriend writes you a love poem, it tends to mean far more than a volume of Keats bought from a bookshop. Those sticky chocolate birthday cakes your mum baked were somehow more enjoyable than those picked up in supermarkets, and a home-made card from a child rarely fails to bring warmth to the heart.

So the next time you have cause to celebrate, allow your creativity to flow. Bake a cake, write a poem, make a compilation of appropriate songs, knit something, take a special photograph, paint a picture, write and sing your own song – you get the idea. Your loved ones will be touched by the amount of time, thought and effort you have put into their celebration gift and they will be thrilled that you care so much. Light a white candle in Jophiel's name and have this burning whenever you are working on your celebration gift to instil it with angel magick and love.

Your creative talents

You are a unique individual and you were born with a unique collection of talents, gifts and attributes. In nurturing these talents and freeing your inspiration, you can lead a life of fulfilment and perhaps even go on to achieve the highest levels of success. At the very least, you will experience joy in your daily life and will feel more productive and worthwhile. However, discovering where your talents lie is half the battle.

It could be that you secretly covet the world of the superstar; that you wish you had the life of Kylie Minogue, Keira Knightley or JK Rowling, but unless you have their talents, drive and determination you are unlikely to achieve their success. However much you might want to be a pop star, if you can't carry a tune in a bucket, all the auditions in the world won't help you. This is because you are trying to sell a talent you simply don't have.

So, how do you discover where your true talents lie? The answer is simple: ask yourself what you are genuinely good at, what you do well, what you are complimented on the most? Also, try to be realistic in your creative aspirations. You are unlikely to become a supermodel if you are short; it is doubtful that you could become a soprano if you are tone deaf. Be good to yourself by being honest with yourself; your confidence and self-respect depend upon your setting goals that you can actually achieve, rather than setting yourself up to fail.

Once you have a clear indication of where your personal talent lies, set about developing it as much as you can. This usually means investing in yourself, so go to night school, drama college or sign up for art classes. It might mean that you require specific coaching and you need to employ a vocal coach or a piano teacher. Or perhaps you need to invest in special tools or equipment so that you can develop your creativity in the comfort of your own home. Once you have done all of this, work the spell on page 183 to help you to nurture your unique gifts.

Spell to nurture your talent

Purpose of ritual: To help you discover and develop your natural talent.

Items required: Pink candle and holder, inscribing tool.

Lunar phase: Full moon.

- ◆ Prepare for ritual in the usual way (see pages 60–1).
- ◆ Spend some time thinking of your creative goals and ambitions and where you would like your talent to take you.
- ◆ Take the candle and inscribe it with the words 'Inspire my creativity' on one side and on the other side 'Nurture my talents'.
- ◆ Place the candle in the holder and light it. Then focus on the flame and begin to chant:

> *Jophiel of talents rare,*
> *I offer up my gift to share.*
> *By the light of the rising star,*
> *Let my talent take me far.*
> *A true proficient I would be,*
> *By angel love, so mote it be.*

- ◆ Keep chanting for as long as you remain focused, then blow out the candle with a wish for success and guidance.
- ◆ Repeat once a week using the same candle, until the candle burns out naturally.
- ◆ Repeat the entire spell as required. To enhance the power of this ritual perform it in conjunction with the scroll of destiny ritual (see page 176).

Lucky break spell

Purpose of ritual: To request a lucky break.

Items required: Tea-light and holder, slip of paper, silver pen, cauldron or heatproof dish.

Lunar phase: New to full moon.

No matter where your creative ambitions lie, no matter what your personal talent is, sometimes all you need is a lucky break: a chance encounter with the boss of the advertising company you want to copy write for, the opportunity to cater a fabulous feast for a friend's low-budget wedding, the chance of being spotted by a talent scout on karaoke night or by a London model agent as you shop for shoes. At some stage in every successful person's career their talent and potential were recognised by someone in the know and they achieved their lucky break. Jophiel can help you to achieve yours.

◆ Take all the items required to your altar and prepare for ritual in the usual way (see pages 60–1).

◆ Place the tea-light in the holder and light it.

◆ Sit for a while and focus on achieving the lucky break you need. Think of how this will change your life in a positive way, then write down on the slip of paper the type of lucky break you need, for example, a publishing deal, the chance to exhibit your artwork or a recording contract.

◆ Light the slip of paper in the flame and allow it to burn in the cauldron. As it burns, say:

> *Herein lies my desire,*
> *Send my dream through the fire.*
> *Jophiel, this spell please take*
> *And bring to me my lucky break.*
> *So mote it be.*

Keep doing all you can to get your talent recognised and remember that persistence is the true key to success.

Just show up!

All talents need to be developed and you need to put the effort in if you wish to become proficient at something. This means playing your chosen musical instrument or sport regularly, it means turning up to dance school even if you have a hangover, it means taking your watercolours out even if the day is damp and cold.

A large proportion of success lies in just showing up. So, instead of declaring to all and sundry that you could write a book, show up at your desk every day and put words on paper. Those people who show up consistently are the ones who earn their lucky break and become truly talented and successful individuals. Be productive, be consistent, work with the angels of inspiration and, above all, enjoy your creativity.

Journey into Summerland

Come with me, my chosen one,
Do not be afraid.
For I will take you to a place
Where the flowers never fade,
To where the grass is always green
And the sky forever blue,
Where the beach is sandy white
And the sea shimmers every hue.
To reach eternal Summerland,
We must journey through the veil,
One final gasp, now reaching out
For a far off light, so pale.
Now move closer to the light,
I'll be with you all the time.
Fear not for your loved ones,
For I will send them all a sign
To let them know that you've moved on
And that you are now at peace,
For I am the angel known as Death
And your spirit I now release.

Into the Light

*A*ngels are all around you, all the time. They can see the daily struggles you go through, the frustrations you endure, the misunderstandings and miscommunications you have with your loved ones. They are witness to the reprimand from your boss – and the drunken night out with friends that follows. They are privy to your nerves during a job interview, your anxiety over your sick relative, your panic and dread as you search in vain for your missing pet.

No aspect of your life is insignificant to the everyday angels; nothing is too small for their compassion, care and celestial assistance. So whether you are up and coming or down and out, flying high or lying low, getting hitched or getting ditched, the angels know all about it and they are there to help you through it.

What follows is a series of everyday angel spells which don't really fit into any of the previous chapters and which are designed to help you through the niggles of daily life. Let's begin with our furry familiars.

Missing pets

When a much-loved pet goes missing, the trauma can be acute. Last year my cat Pyewackett went missing for several days. This was totally out of character for him and I was frantic with worry. I made all the usual telephone calls to vets, shelters and pet shops, I searched the streets and surrounding woodlands looking for him and even rang the local council to see if he had met with a road accident, but there was no sign of him. So I began to work a little magick, both to keep him safe on his adventures and to bring him home as soon as possible. I asked like-minded friends to do the same, creating a web of magick for Pye's safe return. About a week later he came strolling down the garden path, safe and sound and he hasn't strayed since. I still have no idea where he went, but I am thankful to have him safe home again.

If your pet has gone astray – whether it be a dog that has run off or a horse that has been stolen – use the following spells to work towards a safe return.

Spell 1

Light a white candle or tea-light and ask the angels to surround your pet with protective white light, and to guard him from all harm while he is away from home. Ask also that they guide him safely back to you. Repeat daily until your pet returns.

Spell 2

On a slip of paper write the following words, inserting the name of your pet:

> *As I lay in slumber deep,*
> *Let the truth be seen within my sleep.*
> *Uriel reveal to me*
> *Where ---- now may be.*

Repeat the incantation several times before you go to sleep, then place the spell paper under your pillow. Your dream should show you whether or not your pet is safe and when he is likely to return. Be aware though that this ritual cannot guarantee a happy ending.

Spell 3

Light a tea-light and say these words while focusing on the safe return of your pet:

> *Witch to familiar, I call --- to me.*
> *Witch to familiar, --- return to me.*
> *May angels protect you, blessed be,*
> *And guide your steps home to me.*
> *So mote it be.*

Working all three spells daily should give your pet the best possible chance of a safe return. It worked for me and Pyewackett; may it work as well for you.

Lost and found spell

Purpose of ritual: To retrieve what is lost.

Items required: None.

Lunar phase: Any.

It is not only pets that get lost; missing keys, a lost purse and stolen credit cards can all put a cloud over your day. Instead of frantically searching for something, stop, take a deep breath and call for celestial assistance by invoking the help of Chamuel.

◆ Close your eyes and say the following incantation:

> *Angel Chamuel, guide my hand,*
> *That which is lost may now be found.*

◆ Remain silent and keep your eyes closed for a few minutes, then begin to search again, following your intuition and inner guidance. You should soon find whatever it is that you have misplaced.

◆ Say a quick thank you to Chamuel and go about your day.

Family squabbles

Even the closest family members occasionally have their differences of opinion. While some families tend to have a big blazing row, in others the silent treatment is employed to alert family members to their transgressions. Still other families use the sugar-coated venom technique, where it would seem on the surface that all is well, but where the underlying tone suggests otherwise, and interactions are full of snipes, jibes and attempts at putting loved ones on a guilt trip.

Bear in mind during family squabbles that you can only choose your friends, not your family. You were put on this earth with a group of individuals to whom you are emotionally bound and whom you love, but you don't have to like them all, all of the time. There will be occasions when you can't stand the sight of your sister, when parental interest feels like interference, or when your brother's condescending attitude drives you up the wall. It is completely natural to feel that way sometimes, as no family is perfect, however much they might present a united front to the outside world.

Often just removing yourself from the situation is enough to end the dispute. Go for a drive or a walk, or simply end the conversation by saying that you don't wish to argue and you'll talk at a later date. To help the family dynamics adjust and return to normal following a dispute of some kind, try the spell below.

Spell to calm troubled waters

Purpose of ritual: To ease a bad atmosphere following a squabble and to end a dispute.

Items required: White card, scissors, photo of you and one of the family member with whom you have difficulties, glue stick, waterproof pen, plastic tub with a lid, water.

Lunar phase: Full to waning moon.

This is a great spell to ease a dispute and restore a bit of tranquillity to your relationship. It is also very effective if you seem to be having the same old row over and over again, or if a loved one has issues that are repeatedly dragged up. If your big sister has yet to forgive you for cutting the hair off her doll when you were three years old, try this spell!

◆ Prepare for ritual in the usual way (see pages 60–1).

◆ Using the scissors, cut out two (or however many people are involved in the dispute) angel shapes from the card. Cut the faces from the photographs and stick one on each angel shape – you now have one angel to represent yourself and one to represent the family member you are having difficulties with.

◆ Write the nature of the squabble on each angel. If you can, break this down to a key word such as 'jealousy' or 'control'.

◆ Put the angels on your altar and hold your hands over them, palms down, while you say:

> *Guardian angels of my clan,*
> *The circle where my life began,*
> *Stop the squabbles, end the spite,*
> *Cleanse the anger with beams of light.*
> *Moving forth with equal pace,*
> *Bring this family back to grace.*

◆ Place the angels in the tub, fill the tub with water and put on the lid.

◆ Place the whole thing at the back of the freezer to calm and still the troubled waters.

Vehicular angels

For many people, a car represents freedom and independence, not to mention an escape from public transport. But owning a car can bring about its own set of problems and difficulties. Not only are cars expensive to run and maintain, but the sheer number of vehicles on the roads has meant an increase in driver stress levels and incidents of road rage. Add to this, parking problems, car theft and crime, breakdowns and a finance deal that leaves you financially crippled for the next few years, and it is a wonder anyone owns a vehicle.

The fact that so many of us do, however, is proof that the benefits far outweigh the drawbacks. Sometimes, though, it is nice to have a little celestial help as you drive from A to B.

I have already mentioned angelic protection when driving, but some people believe that angels will reserve you a parking space if you ask them to. This may seem silly and an inappropriate use of divine energies, but if being on time to pick the children up from school depends on finding a parking space at the supermarket as quickly as possible then by all means call on the angels. As you set off, ask your angels to provide a quick and easy parking space at your destination.

I personally never drive anywhere without having a quick mental dialogue with my angels first. I always ask for their protection. If I am lost I ask for guidance, if I'm feeling a little nervous due to bad road or weather conditions I ask for peace and tranquillity, and I always ask that they alert me to any hazards in plenty of time. I feel better when my angels are with me as I drive. I feel safer and more confident.

So, the next time you need to drive anywhere, however short a journey, do so with angelic awareness and have a mental dialogue with your guardian angel as you drive. In addition, you can bring the angels to your car in the following ways:

◆ Keep your car keys on an angelic key ring.

◆ Display a bumper sticker that bears an angelic message.

◆ Use a vanilla or lavender in-car air freshener to fill your car with calming, celestial scents.

◆ Visualise angels sitting beside you in the car, on the roof or flying next to the car, looking out for hazards. If nothing else, this will make you smile.

◆ Hang a small angel decoration from your rear view mirror. A yule tree decoration is ideal.

Remember that no job is too big or too small for the angels, so ask for their help in all your vehicular emergencies and dilemmas, and enjoy your motoring skills.

Increasing knowledge

Whoever said that knowledge is power certainly knew what they were talking about. The more you know, the more capable you can become. The more capable you are, the more control you have over your life. And knowledge can even be transformed into money, in that people sometimes sell their talents, unique skills and know-how for a price.

In my opinion, it is ignorance, not poverty, that is the true bane of the masses. Too many children do not receive the education that they deserve, leaving school with inadequate literacy and numeracy skills; too many adults believe that they are too old to learn something new or to brush up an old skill. But for those of you who want the best possible future for yourselves, it is vital that you continuously increase your pool of knowledge, gaining in wisdom, intelligence and the skills you will need to be a success and enjoy your life to the full. Try to develop a basic general knowledge, and an in-depth understanding of the subjects that interest you the most. Improve and broaden your mind with extensive reading, both fact and fiction, and with travel. As you gain in knowledge and broaden your horizons, you will begin to feel more confident and capable, and more in control.

Fortunately, knowledge and information has never been easier to come by, with the internet laying the world open to the intrepid technological explorer. You don't even need to know your way around the web as search engines do most of the work for you. And if, like me, you are a technophobe, you can make full use of the good old-fashioned library.

Library angels ritual

Purpose of ritual: To be guided to the right information at the right time.

Items required: None.

Lunar phase: Any.

The library and the bookshop are halls of learning where information is just waiting to be absorbed by the reader. These days it can be easier and more convenient to visit a website and order books over the internet, but where is the romance in that? At least once every so often you should visit a library or bookshop, allow your eyes to wander across the rows and rows of books and breathe in the fragrance of the printed page. Some larger bookshops even have an internal coffee shop where you can enjoy a latte and a muffin as you flick through the pages of your new purchase.

If you are not sure what you are looking for, have a particular problem you need information about or you are simply browsing in the hope that something wonderful will leap out at you, then call on the library angels to help you. These are the celestial beings of wisdom and knowledge and they can guide you to the right book if you let them.

◆ As you walk into the library or bookshop, silently say the following incantation in your head:

> *Angels of wisdom, dwelling here,*
> *I call your presence from far and near.*
> *Guide me to the book I need,*
> *Increase my knowledge as I read.*
> *So mote it be.*

◆ Stand still for a few moments and then, going on your first instinct, wander to a part of the library or shop. Once in front of the shelves, close your eyes and run your finger along the book spines. When it feels right, stop and open your eyes. Take down the book your finger was on and this should contain the message or information that you need most at this point in your life.

◆ Thank the library angels and take the book home with you.

Living in the light

Hopefully, you are now well on your way to achieving a balanced and magickal life, having called on the angels in all their guises to help you straighten out and heal your health, career, finances and relationships. And, hopefully, you are happy with the changes that you have manifested in your life so far.

When things are going well and your life is moving forwards in a positive direction, you may begin to feel that something is amiss. The fact is that when things are going well, we often can't quite believe our luck and are just waiting for something to go wrong – that unexpected event that pulls the rug from under our feet and leaves us floundering again. As a magickal practitioner, you are aware now that your thoughts have power and that what you focus on you will experience. So, if you think that it's all too good to be true, then it will be. If you expect something to go wrong, then obstacles and difficulties will present themselves accordingly.

Creating a balanced and happy life is really only half the story – now you must maintain it by keeping your thoughts positive. Too many people sabotage their success with negative thoughts, or they shoot themselves in the foot by imagining all that could possibly go wrong. Don't fall into this trap. Maintain a positive attitude towards all aspects of your life and accept that you do deserve to be happy. You deserve to enjoy all the good things that life can offer; you deserve fabulous friendships, pleasant pastimes, a rewarding career, good health, financial and material abundance, romantic interludes and a strong family support system. Just because you may not have all of these things right now does not mean that you do not deserve them, nor does it make you any less worthy of enjoying them when they do manifest in your life.

The angels want you to enjoy your earthly existence. They know that you are a special person and that you have a purpose within the greater tapestry of life. If you open your heart to the celestial beings and attune with them, they will guide you on your true path, helping you to experience joy, success and fulfilment as you brighten the world with your presence, shining like a sparkling diamond as you go through your daily life.

Beyond the rainbow

Somewhere beyond the rainbow, your dreams are waiting to be discovered and turned into reality. Only you will know what these dreams are and how much healing must take place in your life before you are in a position to manifest your deepest desires and claim these dreams as your own. Allow the angels to guide you on this special path, make magick with them regularly, share your hopes and ambitions with them and ask them to lead you forwards in your life to become the best that you can be.

Some day, each and every one of us will be called across the bridge of angels into the Summerland beyond – until then, enjoy every day and strive to live up to your true potential. I hope that the poem below will inspire you to make the very most of every moment. Enjoy!

Rainbow dreams
Now you are over the darkest rainbow of life,
You have cried away sorrow and smiled through strife,
You have travelled the tunnel, come into the light,
You have summoned your strength and reinforced might,
The whole world lies before you, laid out at your feet,
Who knows where you will go, or who you will meet?
As life is renewed, a new journey begins,
Your rising star shines, the Earth slowly spins,
As clouds drift apart, rainbow colours shine bright,
Night's stars softly twinkle your dreams into light.
New horizons now beckon, calling you forth
And you embrace every second, aware of time's worth.

Winging it!

And so we come to the end of our journey together through the celestial dimensions. I hope that the angels have inspired you through these words just as much as they inspired me to write them. Life does not have to be a constant struggle and there are gentle beings of love and light out there whose purpose is to guide and help you. If you close yourself off from this assistance then life can indeed feel like a trial, but if you remain open and trust the angels to assist you in all things, then your life can be truly enchanting.

I hope that as you follow the ways of angel craft you begin to see an all round healing effect taking place in your life, and that the magick and spells laid out in this book engage you and inspire you to take back control and make positive changes with the help of your celestial friends. You are so much more than flesh and blood; you are a radiant being of spirit, at one with the universe, and your purpose here is to light up the world with your unique wisdom, love and light.

Remember that the angels will not do all the work for you. They can help and support you, open up new opportunities for you, but ultimately you still have to put the effort in. This means creating goals for yourself and then doing everything you can to achieve them. It means working magick regularly and being open to new experiences. Above all, it means walking a higher path through life, acknowledging the angels at your side and viewing yourself as a powerful angel healer.

I would like to take this opportunity to thank everyone who has taken the time to write to me over the last few years. I love to hear from my readers, and opening your letters is one of nicest aspects of my job. It's great to hear how my books have helped people, so do feel free to write to me, care of my publisher, and please enclose a stamped self addressed envelope if you would like a reply.

Finally, I would like to wish you well for the future. I hope that we may meet again in future books. Do continue your magickal studies using the Suggested Reading and Resources sections that follow as a guide.

Farewell, my magickal reader. May you live your life forever in the light. Until our next merry meeting, love and bright blessings to you all!

Morgana

Suggested Reading

By the same author

The Witch's Almanac, Quantum/Foulsham, published annually
Candleburning Rituals, Quantum/Foulsham, 2001
Everyday Spells for a Teenage Witch, Quantum/Foulsham, 2002
Faerie Magick, Quantum/Foulsham, 2005
First Steps to Solitary Witchcraft, Quantum/Foulsham, 2005
Fairy Night CD sleeve notes and poetry, New World Music, 2006
How to Create a Magical Home, Quantum/Foulsham, 2006
Workplace Magick, Quantum/Foulsham, 2006
Magical Beasts, Quantum/Foulsham, 2007

Books about angels

Cooney, Denise, *A Plea From the Angels*, Amethyst Books, 1996
Daniel, Alma; Wyllie, Timothy & Ramer, Andrew, *Ask Your Angels*, Piatkus Books, 1992
Eason, Cassandra, *Touched By Angels*, Quantum/Foulsham, 2006
Roland, Paul, *Contact Your Guardian Angel*, Quantum/Foulsham, 2005
Wauters, Ambika, *The Angel Oracle* (divination cards and book), Connections Book Publishing, 1995

Suggested Listening

Musical taste is a very personal thing but here are some of my favourite angel and elemental inspired recordings. They are the perfect background for meditation and ritual.

Cadence, Katie, *On The Wings Of An Angel*, New World Music, 2006
Jones, Stuart, *Touched By Angels*, New World Music, 2006
Rhodes, Stephen, *Protected By Angels*, New World Music, 2005
Spero, Patricia, *Fairy Night*, New World Music, 2006

Resources

Below are some useful addresses that may be of interest to you as you progress in your magickal studies.

Airy Fairy

239 London Road
Sheffield S2 4NF
Tel: 0114 2492090
www.airyfairy.org
E-mail: anwen@airyfairy.org
Readers often ask me where they can buy herbs, tools and so on for their magick, and Airy Fairy is just the place. Owned by a lovely young lady called Anwen, the shop also boasts an internal coffee shop, gardens and a programme of magickal and mystical workshops. Anwen goes to great lengths to verify the ethical source of all her stock and she sells a range of fair trade, organic and cruelty-free gifts and magick products. The shop also offers a mail order service.

Children of Artemis

BM Artemis

London WC1 N3XX

www.witchcraft.org

Children of Artemis produce the *Witchcraft and Wicca* magazine and organise pagan events, including the popular Witchfest festivals, throughout the UK.

Dark Angel Designs

7 Town Hall Street

Sowerby Bridge

West Yorkshire

HX6 2QD

www.thedarkangel.co.uk

This company specialises in making fairytale clothing for men, women and children.

New World Music Ltd

Harmony House

Hillside Road East

Bungay

Suffolk NR35 1RX

www.newworldmusic.com

New World Music produces some amazing albums of magickal music, often with well known writers creating the informative sleeve notes. They offer a great mail order service.

About the Author

Marie Bruce is a best-selling author, journalist and published poet. She is a practising solitary witch and she has written several books on various aspects of the craft, some of which have been translated into foreign language editions. She is a full member of The Society of Authors.

As a member of The National Union of Journalists, Marie has contributed to various magazines and newspapers, including *Prediction* and *Witchcraft and Wicca*. She has also authored several home-study courses for The Regent Academy, and has created extensive sleeve notes and poetry for New World Music.

Through her work, Marie is known for her down-to-earth accessibility, Wiccan wisdom, personal anecdotes and sassy feminine wit. She lives in Yorkshire with her familiar, a cat named Pyewackett. There she spends her time writing, reading, horse-riding, singing and dancing and, of course, spellcasting.

She has been described as 'a Wiccan icon' and 'the official witch of England'.

Marie's books can be ordered direct from www.foulsham.com

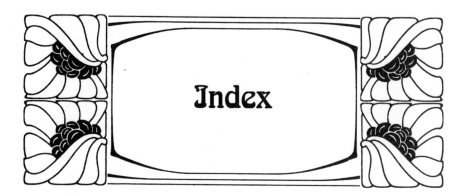

Index

Major page references are in **bold** –
Spells/rituals are in *italics*